FIRST:

Sensual Lesbian Stories of New Beginnings

First:
Sensual Lesbian Stories of New Beginnings

Edited by Cheyenne Blue

CONTENTS

INTRODUCTION

Everyone remembers their first time.

Of course, we are constantly experiencing firsts in our lives, right from the very first breath as a newborn. First day at school, leaving home for the first time, first time to climb a mountain, first kiss. First time to fall in love. First lovemaking. Oh yes, first love, the most heady first of all. That most people will experience at least some of these things in their lives doesn't make them any less memorable.

This is an anthology of lesbians and first times. But don't be fooled—these are not just stories of first-time lesbian experience. There *are* some very fine stories with that theme in here, but this collection takes a broad sweep across the landscape of first times.

Annabeth Leong's tale of a woman's first boxing match plunges you straight in, with all the physical and emotional ramifications of that heady new experience. Jeremy Edwards delights with a bawdy story set in 1920s Hollywood when the first "Talkies" made an appearance. Andi Marquette and Jillian Boyd contribute emotional tales of love as a step along the way to two very different kinds of healing, while Emily L. Byrne's tale of a woman forced to hand over the keys of her house to an antagonistic ex-lover adds a bittersweet twist. If you want to read stories of first time lesbian experience, Tamsin Flowers' story of a curious straight woman, and Vanessa de Sade's tale of first love unfolding in 1970s Scotland will hit the spot.

This introduction wouldn't be complete without an acknowledgement of another first: Rosie Bower, Brenda Murphy, and Ivy Newman make their debuts in this collection as published writers.

From first time writers to seasoned pros, the fifteen stories in *First: Sensual Lesbian Stories of New Beginnings* offer sensual and imaginative takes on the theme from the very first page.

Cheyenne Blue
Queensland, Australia

ROSES AND THORNS
ANNABETH LEONG

"Are you sure you want to get in the ring?" Arlene asked.

Ruth ignored her girlfriend and concentrated on tying back her long, brown hair. It wasn't the first time this question had come up. She watched herself in the mirror, focusing on the fuzzy pink bands she'd bought in deference to women's boxing regulations—hair had to be fastened with something soft. She didn't let her gaze flick to Arlene's face.

"I mean," Arlene continued, "I remember what you said about your dad."

Ruth's nostrils flared. She'd expected him to be proud when she'd told him about signing up for classes at the boxing gym. He'd been the one to push her to play sports when she was younger—back then, she'd preferred books and dolls. She'd thought her dad would understand when she explained how good it felt to cut loose on the bag, to be strong and take up space, to let go of her fears that someone might get hurt.

Just don't get in the ring, he'd said instead. *Broken noses aren't pretty.*

"I really want to do this, Arlene," Ruth said—calmly, quietly. She had the voice of a church choir soloist. She'd seen herself entirely as that girl, too, until months of drills had tuned her into a taut power that buzzed beneath pale skin made soft by peach-scented lotion and cheeks that blushed when Arlene told dirty jokes.

The gym manager snapped into the dressing room. "Fifteen minutes, ladies!" The murmur of conversation around them intensified.

Ruth nodded, let go of her hair, and began wrapping her knuckles. She'd paid extra for pretty strips of cloth. Roses and thorns. It had taken so long for her to realize that even the most beautiful flowers could wield weapons. Now she wanted to be sure she never forgot.

"I saw the other girl," Arlene said. "She looks big. Right at the top of your weight class, I bet."

Ruth sighed, tucked in the ends of her wraps, and turned to Arlene. Her tough, tattooed girlfriend had first caught her eye with a butch swagger to die for, but now she fretted and paced. She tripped over the half-spilled contents of another girl's backpack. The familiar smells of sweat and rubber training mats focused Ruth, but Arlene didn't seem to notice them.

"I'm going to be fine," Ruth told her, but Arlene didn't even pause. Ruth stepped closer, bumping her hip with a wrapped hand. "I'm going to be fine," she repeated.

"That other girl is going to hit you," Arlene said.

Ruth laughed. "And you can cheer when I hit her back."

Arlene ducked her head, the gesture boyish. "I'm sorry," she said. "I'm being a jerk. I know you've been practicing."

"Including sparring, you know. I've had fists coming at me before."

"This seems different. I keep thinking of that movie—"

"Oh Jesus. She's not going to hit me in the spine or whatever you're worrying about."

"I know." Arlene's face was shadowed. All Ruth could make out was the line of her pressed-together lips.

"I need you to trust me."

"I know." Arlene lifted her head slowly. Her eyes were open wide, and they made her look much younger than usual. Even the patch of light scars across her dark cheek—from a dog bite, though Ruth knew she liked people to think she'd gotten them in a fight—made her seem tender and vulnerable.

Ruth nodded, because at least Arlene was trying. Her dad, on the other hand, had said he couldn't bear to watch this bout. Then Arlene leaned forward and kissed Ruth as if she was the most precious thing in the world, her hard mouth soft, and her strong tongue gentle.

It did feel good to be loved like that, but Ruth couldn't help but notice a curl of distaste in her stomach. Her muscles ached to contract and release, to reach for and find their limits, to pound and be pounded. She pulled away from Arlene, stroking wrapped knuckles along her jaw. "You should probably grab your seat." The moment Ruth walked into the ring, she wanted to be a fighter head to toe. She couldn't be that woman while her girlfriend kept looking at her like she might break.

* * *

It made Ruth nervous that she wasn't nervous. As the least experienced fighter in the lineup, she had the first bout of the night. Other girls from her gym gave her a few last-minute tips, but mostly they recognized that she wanted everyone out of her way. With Arlene and her dad so concerned, she felt as if she ought to be worried about bruising or broken noses or just looking stupid. Instead, she adjusted her protective gear and marveled at the peaceful feeling in the center of her chest. Was she totally delusional? She felt so sure she could handle this. Why didn't anyone else seem to think so?

Ruth flexed her calves and looked at them. They'd transformed since she'd started jumping rope as part of the drills at the gym. She'd always had a generous, voluptuous body, so her legs hadn't grown in size. She wondered if Arlene could feel the change, though. When Ruth hugged her and wrapped a leg behind her thighs, did she know that Ruth was thinking about knocking her to the ground with one smooth sweep, following her down, and pinning her until she kissed her breathless?

The gym manager reappeared. She was a wiry, ivory-skinned woman who'd been a pro before giving birth to four children in six years. She clapped Ruth on the shoulder. "Three rounds. You ready for this?"

Ruth nodded, slipping her mouthguard in.

"You scared?"

Ruth shook her head.

"Good. The way you punch, she ought to be saying her prayers."

Grinning fiercely around the bulky mouthguard, Ruth felt like a star. She knew this gym, but everything seemed different now that she was participating in an official bout. Pictures on the walls of Marlen Esparza, Nicola Adams, and the gym's collection of contenders no longer seemed like simple inspiration. She was about to be initiated into their ranks, even if only in a small way.

She followed the manager to the ring. About half the crowd was familiar—the women who trained here. The other half were significant others, bored teenagers, or parents. Ruth scanned the other women, noting how some seemed uncomfortable while others glanced toward her with sparkling eyes. Some of them would probably be signing up as soon as the matches were over. One woman looked like she thought she ought to be out of place— but Ruth saw her, discovering fists at the sides of her flowery dress. She met her eyes and smiled.

Beyond her was Arlene. Now that she was more in public, she had her tough face back on. She'd shoved her hands into the pockets of low-slung jeans, subtly showing off well-developed arms bared by her tight-fitting tank top. Only Ruth knew that the sexy mussed effect of her hair had been caused by nervously rubbing the back of her head. She looked away quickly before the expression of doubt on Arlene's face could knock her out of her fighter's mindset again.

The manager welcomed everyone to the evening's event, explained the rules, and introduced Ruth and her opponent, Johnette. When the signal came, Ruth ducked smoothly into the ring. Her body felt *good*—so lithe and mobile. Someone had gotten the idea to have thong-clad men walk around the ring to hype the crowd for each round, and Ruth smiled indulgently as the crowd whooped and hollered for the oiled-up boytoy who had been selected.

Then the buzzer rang, and she saw nothing but Johnette. More accurately, she saw Johnette as a collection of threats, obstacles, and targets. Arms and shoulders that would parry, gloved fists that would punch, nimble feet that would carry her out of reach or sneak her in close. A head that would duck and weave. Narrowed eyes that studied Ruth in turn, breaking her down and searching out all the same things.

Bare of makeup, Johnette's face was stark and shadowed. With a shock, Ruth realized she must look that way, too. She clenched her fists inside her gloves, and thought of a rose's thorns rather than its petals. Planting herself firmly in her stance, she felt her body lining up into a posture she had practiced enough to make automatic.

Halfway through Ruth's deep breath, Johnette darted in tight. A light flurry of blows landed on Ruth's stomach, testing the distance between them more than aiming to hurt. With a start, Ruth remembered to move.

She had problems, she knew, with telegraphing her intentions as she wound up a punch, but there was no helping that now. Ruth steeled herself through more blows as she hauled off and landed a heavy cross on the side of Johnette's headgear. It had been a surprise to learn that she fought with the slow, hard-hitting blows of a brawler. Ruth had grown up with a more delicate vision of herself. This punch, though—it *landed*. Shockwaves rippled up her wrist and into her elbow, and the solidity of it all felt incredible. Johnette's body gave way before Ruth's arm. The other woman's feet faltered, and she stumbled back.

A cry went up from the crowd, Arlene's voice clear in the mix, and the sound spurred Ruth forward. She punched once more. Twice. Johnette reeled. Ruth's pulse surged.

The other woman hadn't lost her speed, though. Suddenly, she wasn't where Ruth had lined up to strike. Punches seemed to come from both sides of Ruth's head at once, jabs and hooks that startled the breath from her and made her muscles ache with impending bruises. She had landed only three hits, each one heavy and significant, but now she struggled to find a way to regroup and launch another strong attack.

The buzzer rang. How had it been two minutes already? Ruth backed up and shook her head. Had she been fighting fast or slow? Across the ring, Johnette looked similarly dazed. Ruth's sternum ached from the heaving of her chest. Her hands felt sticky inside the gloves, inside her wraps. She accepted water, but her breathing hadn't returned to normal by the time the buzzer rang to signal the start of round two.

She was tired already. All her drills should have protected her from that, and yet her fists were so heavy it was hard to keep them up to guard her face. Johnette rushed in, and for the first time in her life, Ruth felt what it was like for someone to come at her without holding back at all. Johnette clearly didn't see flower petals when she looked at Ruth. A dull red mark beside the strap of her tank top revealed one spot where Ruth's fist had fallen. Johnette was a blinding fury of fists. Ruth fell back before her.

Light as the other woman was on her feet, Arlene had been right about her size. She had several pounds on Ruth, and could easily have had more. Ropes snapped against Ruth's back. Each time Ruth lifted her fists, blows around her upper arms made them drop back down. Johnette hit Ruth's chin, making her teeth clench around her mouthguard.

She was pretty sure she was losing. Maybe her dad and Arlene had been right—she wasn't tough enough for this after all.

Her ears picked up a sound, though, distinct even amid the noise of the crowd. Johnette was panting as if her chest was about to burst. Ruth shook her head slowly, and again she didn't feel nervous or scared or upset to be getting hurt. She'd have plenty of bruises later, that was for sure, but this was nothing she couldn't handle.

She ignored Johnette's blows and settled into her stance again, trying to bring back that vision of her opponent as a set of threats, obstacles, and targets. Blows landed, but they weren't rocking her yet. To discourage her adversary, Ruth put out a fist. She didn't strike from the arm—this punch came from her hip and her knee and the floor beneath her. Johnette gasped and fell back, and Ruth stepped forward.

Now she found a rhythm. Johnette landed mosquito stings, but Ruth was a big beast. She could take bug bites, especially when every blow she landed rocked the other woman. Something came over her, a need, a drive. She wanted to hit and hit, and Johnette's returned strikes seemed so insignificant.

The buzzer rang.

Someone was screaming Ruth's name. Blinking sweat out of her eyes, she turned and saw Arlene, pressed to the front of the crowd, pumping her fist like she was at a concert. Ruth gulped down more water, but she couldn't shake her awareness of Arlene, wild for her.

The third and final round. Ruth knew what to do now. She couldn't feel anything, and that turned out to be almost like feeling everything. Breath rushed in past her nostrils and filled her chest entirely. Her calves flexed. Her sides ached along her ribs. Her biceps contracted. Her gloves compressed between her knuckles and Johnette's body. She felt invincible. She landed more blows, and she sort of remembered to do footwork at the same time. She didn't parry as much as she'd been taught to do, but it barely felt like she needed to.

It was a surprise to find herself suddenly on her back. Johnette hit her a certain way at the side of her head, and Ruth fell neatly. There was counting, and more screaming. Twisting her head to one side, the vinyl mat sticky against her cheek, Ruth glanced past the ropes and saw Arlene. Her girlfriend hadn't stopped shouting her name. She was sweating as if she were the one in the ring. And Ruth could tell she believed now. She saw the fighter Ruth wanted to be.

The knowledge lifted her to her feet. This bout was almost over, and despite how heavily Ruth's blows landed when she launched them, Johnette had outmaneuvered her. None of that mattered, though. The counting stopped, and Ruth knew she had another glorious minute to be this new person.

She hit hard and felt strong, and she fed on Johnette's fear of her and respected her power in return. She found the ragged edge of her body's endurance, and she played there, alive in a way she had rarely been. When the buzzer rang the final time, she sagged with equal parts exhaustion and satisfaction.

The manager stepped into the ring and lifted Johnette's gloved hand high, but Ruth looked at Arlene and grinned as if she'd won the victory.

* * *

Arlene pressed a towel to Ruth's sweating forehead, the gesture gentle and maternal. Ruth batted her hand away. "I should get back out there. Watch the other bouts."

They were alone in the dressing room, the scent of Ruth's sweat sharp and strong around them. Bruises were rising all over her skin. Despite that and the lack of makeup, she'd never felt prettier. Ruth pushed herself up from the chair she'd been sitting in, catching a glimpse of her movement in the mirror. Was there such a thing as a dainty swagger? If so, she'd found it.

"Wait," Arlene said. She caught Ruth by the wrist.

The touch was so light compared to all Ruth had endured, and yet the breath whooshed out of Ruth's chest and for a second she felt the way she had just before Johnette had knocked her down.

"Yeah?"

Arlene ran her tongue over her top teeth, head cocked to one side. "Fuck, I don't know how to say it."

"What?"

"You... Fuck."

Ruth started to laugh, but Arlene cut her off with a hard, demanding kiss. The kiss *hurt*, stretching a jaw that Ruth had only just discovered was sore, crushing her against Arlene's chest and revealing that breast protectors hadn't worked as well as she might have hoped. Arlene never kissed her like this, and it seemed even less likely that she would do it now, when she could surely see Ruth's bruises.

Ruth couldn't sink into the kiss because she kept expecting it to end. Any second now, she thought, Arlene would pull back and check to make sure she was okay.

Arlene released Ruth's mouth, but didn't say anything. Instead, she stared at Ruth with a hungry expression that Ruth had never seen before. She grabbed big handfuls of Ruth's hair and yanked them, pulling

Ruth's head back. Arlene brought her teeth to the very top of Ruth's neck and bit harder than she ever had.

Ruth yelped in surprise, jerking in Arlene's grasp, but Arlene only growled. Ruth whimpered, and her whole body pulsed with the sound. She inched forward and found Arlene's thigh waiting, ready to slip beneath her legs.

Her clit was a bruise, tender but full of fascinating sensations. She couldn't help pressing into the ache of it.

Ruth's bruises followed the lead of her clit. Everywhere her body contacted Arlene's, the bruises throbbed.

Arlene released Ruth's throat to the sting of cool air. "Fuck," she said. "You can take it like this, can't you? You can really fucking take it."

It was Ruth's turn to growl. "I was trying to tell you."

"I know."

Another time they would have talked about that more, but Ruth was busy grabbing Arlene's hand and forcing it into her boxing shorts, below the belt where she knew any blow would really count.

Arlene's knee knocked the chair as she repositioned them frantically, but she didn't even pause to curse. She pressed Ruth against the nearest wall, yanking her tank top and sports bra up and shoving her boxing shorts and panties to her knees. Her hip banged Ruth's pelvis. Her thigh already had the rhythm, pressing so hard against Ruth's crotch that she almost lifted her off the floor.

"Fuck me," Ruth commanded, her voice no longer the choir soloist's.

She didn't feel precious or fragile. She felt durable, ready to take everything Arlene could offer and then some. Ruth grabbed Arlene's strong deltoids for purchase, but there was an answering contraction in her own deltoids, her own muscles.

ROSES AND THORNS

Arlene's fingers slipped into Ruth's wet cunt, and Ruth had to mirror the gesture, shoving Arlene's leg out of the way and seeking the wetness between her thighs. It was violent. Ruth drove her hand in the way she'd been taught to land an uppercut. Working her thrust from the hips also forced her farther onto Arlene's seeking fingers. She pulled her lover into a clinch, forehead against forehead. She wanted to fuck and get fucked, but she didn't want to be the first to give in.

"Are you going to come for me?" Ruth's voice was hoarse.

"Fuck. Are *you* going to come for *me?*"

"Only if you make me."

Those were fighting words, destined to strike the heart of Arlene's pride. Normally, Arlene wouldn't have fought her, but now neither of them could stop. Arlene's cunt squeezed Ruth's fingers as if trying to force them out, but Ruth pressed higher and harder, the muscles of her forearms trembling. The crushing heat of her lover's cunt ground her knuckles together, but she felt she could come from the rush of fighting back.

Arlene didn't apply any of her usual finesse. She wasn't searching for Ruth's most sensitive spots. She just pushed deep, big knuckles getting stuck at Ruth's entrance and banging crudely against it.

Shifting out of the clinch, Arlene's lips whispered over Ruth's cheeks, but she didn't kiss. Finding the root of Ruth's jaw, she bit again. Ruth cried out, then bit her lip. The gym wasn't a big place. If she started screaming, someone would probably hear it.

Into the new silence, Arlene bit harder.

The effort of holding her breath tightened every one of Ruth's muscles. She tried to fight it still, to keep her hand moving inside Arlene, to resist the pleasure—she wasn't sure if coming now would make her strong or weak. After a few moments, though, she no longer had a choice. Her body cared nothing for certain battles. Sensation burst from where Arlene held her and rushed through her, rattling her bones, reaching every one of her bruises.

She couldn't help making noise, either, but Arlene's mouth found hers, and as she swallowed Ruth's noises, Ruth felt her girlfriend's body also begin to pulse.

The pleasure fell away slowly, leaving behind a stronger ache than the bruises had on their own. Ruth eased her fingers out of Arlene, and Arlene did the same. They met each other's eyes, and Ruth felt her face heat, as if Arlene had not seen her this way many times before. "Fuck," Ruth said. Arlene nodded as if in simple agreement.

There was so much Ruth wanted to say—about being pretty and about being strong, about being loved and being challenged. About what it felt like to strip away her makeup and risk breaking her nose. About standing her ground and giving as good as she got.

Now wasn't the time. Instead, she yanked her clothes back into place and leaned forward to give Arlene a simmering promise of a kiss. Her heart pounded, and she liked the idea of standing in the crowd smelling of sex and sweat, reliving her own bout as she watched other women fight. "Let's get back out there," she said.

THE OPPOSITE OF DARKNESS
HARPER BLISS

"Ready?" Doctor Matheson asked.

Erica had grown close to the man over the past year. And now he was about to give her the one thing she'd never believed she'd have again. Her sight.

Everyone was here. Lauren squeezed her right hand. Her mother did the same with her left. Erica heard her father expel some agitated breaths from a corner of the room and, although she couldn't see her—yet—she sensed Jenny's presence at the end of the bed.

"I've been ready for seven years, Doc," Erica replied. Seven years of darkness is a long time. Seven years during which so much had changed and she hadn't seen any of it. Erica remembered what her parents looked like, of course. Her dad's gruff forehead with the deep worry lines. Her mother's button nose and ever-shifting gaze. But she'd never seen Jenny's or Lauren's faces. She had an image in her head of what Lauren, her partner of the past four years, looked like, and she'd let her fingers flit over her face almost every day of their life together, but she'd never actually seen her. Not with her eyes.

"Do we really want our parents in the room when we first meet?" Erica had asked Lauren before the surgery.

"Don't be silly, babe," Lauren had whispered in her ear. "We met years ago."

Erica knew Lauren hadn't said that to brush off any concerns. She'd said it because it was true.

"As we discussed before, everything will be blurry at first, and it will take some time before objects truly come into focus," Doctor Matheson said. "It can take months before vision is fully restored."

"Yes." Erica nodded. She'd waited long enough. "I'm ready."

In the few seconds it took the doctor to bring his hands to her eyes and start peeling off the bandages, the past seven years flashed through Erica's mind. The accident. Cory leaving when Erica needed her most. Hiring Jenny to help her adjust to life as a vision-impaired person. Jenny introducing her daughter, Lauren, to Erica. And now this.

It had taken numerous surgeons seven years to amass the knowledge—and work up the nerve—to accomplish this. But now, after seven years of only sound and smell and taste and touch, Erica would be able to employ her fifth sense again.

She'd often discussed with Jenny if it was worse to be born blind and never to have seen and hence not know what you'd been missing, or to become blind, and have all the images stored in your memory, but not be able to add new ones, or see the old ones again. It was a never-ending discussion, with arguments in favor of both cases depending on Erica's mood, but most of the time she was glad that she'd been able to see before. Even though it didn't make the darkness easier to deal with.

Erica felt the bandage over her left eye loosen as Doctor Matheson slowly removed it. Lauren's fingers wound themselves a little tighter around Erica's.

Erica kept her eyes closed—she wanted to open both eyes at once. Doctor Matheson started on the other bandage, repeating the process. That was when the nerves really hit her. Everything would change again. What if the surgery hadn't been entirely successful? What if she only got her vision back for a day, or a few weeks? What if some other mistake had occurred? Because, as Erica well knew, accidents happened.

"Okay, Erica," the doctor said. "Slowly open your eyes. Take your time. There's no rush."

Erica was determined not to let her newly acquired vision be blurred by tears. She'd done enough crying. If anything, this was a time for smiling. She hadn't seen the reflection of her own smile in years. Then again, she hadn't had that much reason for smiling. Not the first few years, anyway. Not until Jenny and Lauren saved her not only from the physical darkness she'd been dumped in, but also from the encroaching mental darkness that was starting to take more than her ability to see. The one that was chipping away at her ability to live.

There's no such thing as slowly opening your eyes. Either they're open or they're closed. So Erica opened her eyes, and blinked a few times. She saw light. A few dark, smudged shapes. But it didn't matter what she saw, as long as she was seeing something.

Everyone around her had gone quiet. Were they waiting for her to say something? Something meaningful, perhaps? Or for her to confirm that the surgery had been a success? But Erica wanted to remain in that moment a few seconds longer. The moment the world presented itself to her again, in light, and color, and shadows—and reverent silence.

"I can see," she said, still blinking, her brain trying to adjust to her retinas absorbing and translating light into images—just shadowy shapes, really, but images nonetheless.

"What do you see, honey?" her mother asked.

"Just..." But Erica couldn't describe it. She'd no longer have any need of other people describing themselves to her, either. Like Lauren had, on Erica's request, when they'd first met.

"Which celebrity do you look like? It needs to be

15

someone who was famous before my accident." She'd sat there grinning like a fool, because Lauren's voice was low and sexy and her energy when she entered Erica's flat had done something to her. It had been a blatant set-up by Jenny, who had said, after giving Erica the tough love she needed those first few difficult months, "I know you and I know my daughter. Believe me, this will be a match made in heaven."

"But I'm blind," Erica had said. It had been enough reason for Cory to leave, although that wasn't entirely accurate. Erica's attitude had greatly contributed to Cory's decision for them to "go on a break."

"So?" was all Jenny had replied. It was her go-to response when Erica was feeling sorry for herself.

"I don't look like anyone famous," Lauren had said. "I'm just me."

"Oh, come on. Meet me halfway here," Erica had insisted. "I know *I* have some Sandra Bullock in me."

They'd both broken out in giggles and it was never established whom Lauren resembled.

Soon Erica would be able to see for herself. Soon, when this blurriness made way for more defined pictures. For now, she could make out the blueish hue of the sky behind the flimsy hospital curtains. And the hulking outline of her father on the far side of the room .

"You don't need to say anything, babe." Lauren reassured her. "You have all the time in the world to process and talk about this. All the time in the world." She leaned over—and Erica actually saw Lauren's torso approaching, instead of just sensing a shift in the air— and kissed Erica on the top of her head.

Erica brought her hand to Lauren's face; let a finger slide along her cheek. She'd established long ago that she had high cheekbones, and a strong chin, but she couldn't feel the color of her eyes—coffee brown, she'd been told—or the shade of pink of her lips.

Erica would have to remain in the hospital for observation a few days longer, but once she got home, she knew what she'd be doing first. Taking in the colors of Lauren. Laying eyes on the freckle on her inner thigh that Lauren liked to guide her finger toward. Determine whether her hair was ash-blond or dirty blond or just plain blond. See her appendectomy scar instead of just letting a fingertip skate across it.

* * *

"What have you done to my apartment?" Erica said when she and Lauren arrived home. It had taken another week before Doctor Matheson had allowed her to be discharged from under his watch. In that week, everything she saw had become more distilled. When she'd watched the news on TV the presenter had, incrementally as the days progressed, transformed from a gray and pink blob into an actual person. Erica *had* cried then. When she'd first been able to make out the contours of another human being's body in all its details, she hadn't been able to keep the image from becoming blurry again. But that was only temporary, and at least that way she'd already shed her tears by the time a real person came to visit her. That person was Lauren.

"Just made it a bit prettier." Lauren had quite quickly moved into the apartment Erica used to share with Cory. Now, though, they'd finally be able to move somewhere else. Somewhere Erica didn't have to feel her way around. Somewhere she didn't know everything by touch.

"I guess I never realized you have questionable taste," Erica joked, casting her eyes around the living room where she had spent the last decade of her life. A vase filled with tulips now stood where Cory's rather ridiculous toy soldier collection used to be. Everything that had belonged to Cory had been replaced by Lauren's belongings. Erica knew this, of course, but witnessing this change with her own eyes for the first time made her go a bit soft on the inside regardless.

"And I guess your lack of vision made you miss the past years' evolution in interior design," Lauren replied. It was exactly this sort of take-no-prisoners humor that had made Erica fall for Lauren. After she'd stopped wallowing in her misery, someone like Lauren by her side had been what she needed. Jenny *had* been right.

"Can't wait to see what you've done to our bedroom, babe." Erica dropped her bag and shrugged off her coat. As overwhelming as it was to come home and to be able to see her apartment again, it wasn't nearly as urgent as the heat building in her blood. Since the first second she'd truly been able to make out Lauren's contours—those alpine cheekbones, that curve of her hip—she'd only been able to think about coming home and feasting her eyes on *all* of her lover. She wanted her naked before it went dark. For Erica, it was essential to have daylight streaming in through the windows when she looked at Lauren's intimate parts for the very first time. Artificial light would simply not do.

"Come on." Lauren grabbed her by the hand and dragged her in the right direction. Moving through the apartment unencumbered was also a freeing experience, and it only made Erica's desire grow bolder.

Strangely, Lauren always slept with a sleep mask covering her eyes. She had one hanging from the bedpost at all times and as they came to a stop by the bed, Lauren presented it to Erica and said, "I thought I'd blindfold you."

Erica snatched the mask from Lauren's hands and tossed it to the floor, but not without wondering if she would ever be able to sleep in a non-pitch black environment. At the hospital, sleep had been elusive at best since the bandages had been removed. Erica had drifted in and out of it, exhausted by all the emotions and the new sensations, day and night, not caring that a hospital room rarely went dark. She didn't want darkness, anyway. All she'd wanted was the opposite of it.

"You'd best lay off the dark humor and strip, babe. I've never been more ready in my life." Erica's hands reached for a button of Lauren's blouse and she couldn't help herself—she had to start tugging, had to start undoing clothes, had to see naked skin. She'd felt every inch of that skin, had explored it for hours with her fingertips, her cheeks, her tongue, but now she was ready to examine it with her eyes as well.

"What? No gentle lovemaking? And here I was thinking this would be a tantric experience. The pair of us at opposite ends of the room just staring at each other until we couldn't take it anymore." Lauren grinned. She had a bit of Michelle Pfeiffer in her when she cracked a crooked smile like that.

"As far as I'm concerned, this is our first time. One I've waited a very long time for."

"Oh, I see. The chastity belt has finally come off." Lauren pulled her close by the neck and kissed her.

This must be exciting for her as well, Erica thought. *To surrender to my gaze for the very first time.* This did not quiet Erica's lust. Their kiss grew frantic, their lips mashing together, their tongues meeting in a darting frenzy.

"Fuck, you're so hot," Erica said, slightly out of breath, when they came up for air. "Like... what's her name... from that TV show." But Erica didn't have a brain that remembered faces, nor TV shows for that matter. Seven years without vision also had left her quite oblivious to today's ridiculous body standards and fashion hypes. Lauren might as well have walked around in nothing but sweat pants for the entire time Erica couldn't see. Nonetheless, she'd dressed up today—for the day she was taking a seeing Erica home. She wore a baby blue blouse tucked into a tight pair of jeans, and

19

Erica thought that, perhaps, that was one of the things she had missed the most. To see a woman fully clothed one instant, and stark naked the next. The contrast. The urgency. The desire displayed in the seconds the clothes came off.

"Téa Leoni?" Lauren asked.

"I don't even know who that is." Erica pulled Lauren close again, but instead of kissing her, she flipped open a few more buttons of her blouse. A navy blue bra with lace skirting the cups peeked through. Erica didn't recall ever coming across much lace among Lauren's undergarments. She must have gone shopping for the occasion. Meanwhile, Erica had had no choice but to wear the comfortable clothing she'd gone into hospital with. And the same old beige bra, of which she'd never known the color before. After this—perhaps a few days of this—a shopping trip was in order.

Erica dragged her finger along the skin above Lauren's bra—just like before, but entirely different at the same time. Before, she would have used her finger to gain arousal *and* information. Now, it was purely for arousal. Erica already knew what the slope of Lauren's breast felt like, but the sight of it curving out of that bra cup left her gasping for air.

"Hey." Lauren put her hand over Erica's. "How about we take it slow? All this visual stimulation will have you climaxing in minutes, otherwise."

Erica already felt her clit pulsing against her panties, and her nipples poking hard against the fabric of her bra. "Yes." She nodded and took a deep breath. Her hand was still on Lauren's breast, and her eyes—her eyes were everywhere. Her gaze flitted from the unruly curl on the side of Lauren's head, to the three freckles on her nose, to the hollow of her neck, and the promise of her half-open blouse.

Lauren loosened her grasp on Erica's hand and

trailed her fingers over it. "Why don't you sit back and... watch," she said.

Erica's lips curved into a grin. She didn't need a mirror—or the power of eyesight—to know it was a leery, horny grin. "Oh yes." She took a few steps toward the bed and sat. Out of habit, her hands touched the mattress before she allowed her bottom to crash down. "A striptease." Before she'd lost her vision, Erica would have scoffed at the idea, but now, it made her flesh sizzle—and feel very constrained underneath her clothes despite their comfortable nature.

Lauren sank her teeth into her bottom lip and proceeded to open the buttons Erica hadn't got to yet. She let the sides of her blouse hang open while trailing a finger from between her collarbones, down the cleft of her cleavage, over her belly button to the button of her jeans, which she undid painfully slowly, her gaze locked on Erica's.

Most of all, Erica thought, *it's her eyes*. Oh, what she had missed not being able to look into her partner's eyes.

"You want more?" Lauren asked.

Erica failed to reply. She couldn't. Her throat was so dry, she feared she might choke if she tried to speak. Heat traveled through her veins. Her panties were damp against her ever-swelling pussy lips. So instead, she simply nodded.

Lauren pushed her jeans off her legs. Her panties matched her bra. A thin strip of lace edged the waistband and the blue looked so delicious against the porcelain of her skin, it made Erica's mouth water. Lauren had been wrong. This was already too much. She needed that frantic, early release Lauren had alluded to earlier. Not only because regaining her vision and seeing her lover on full display rendered her beyond hot, but also because of all the pent-up emotions that were clawing their way free of her soul. Most of all, she needed to see. Now.

"Take off your bra, please," she pleaded, her voice hoarse and low.

Lauren obliged and let her blouse slip from her arms. Erica watched as it landed in a puddle of light blue on the bedroom's hardwood floor. Lauren brought her hands behind her back and held her bra up for a brief moment before sending Erica a warm smile, and letting it tumble down the same path her blouse had taken. She stood with her hands at her sides, her gaze on Erica, but Erica, for the first time, averted her eyes from Lauren's. She knew the shape of Lauren's breasts, of course. The size of her nipples. But she'd only ever heard about the light-brown birthmark the shape of Asia to the side of her right breast. And the color pink she'd imagined Lauren's nipples to be was much darker than reality. They pointed upward in the most arousing display of lust. Erica realized that conjuring an image of breasts in her mind, no matter how perfect they might be, never lived up to casting her gaze upon the real thing. The mounds heaving with ragged breath. The person they belonged to being the woman who'd entered her life and brightened it beyond the ability to see.

Lauren's hands slid toward her panties and, slowly, she started pushing them down. Her breasts swayed in the process, and then Lauren stood completely naked in front of Erica.

"Oh, christ," Erica muttered. "You are so unbelievably beautiful." It was doubly true, because for the longest time Erica had believed she'd never see her partner like this.

"Oh, but so are you, babe," Lauren said, and came for her. "Fuck, I want you naked too." She tugged at Erica's sweater and it came off easily. No striptease required.

Erica got up and stepped out of her panties, unclasped her bra and tossed it as far away from her as possible—she'd never wear that particular one again. By the time all her clothes had gone, Lauren had lain down on the bed in front of her, her knees clasped together chastely.

Erica wasn't having any of that. She moved onto the bed and kneeled in front of Lauren's closed legs. She put her hands on Lauren's knees and gently pushed them apart. Erica had seen plenty of lady parts before things became serious with Cory, but she'd never seen Lauren's. And now, at last, her gaze was fixed on Lauren's pussy. Gleaming lips. Wetness already spread to her upper thighs. A neatly trimmed bush. Before she'd lost her sight, she'd been too young to have lovers with gray hairs down there, but Lauren had a few lighter threads running through the curls on her mound. Her clit protruded the tiniest of bits.

Erica had been told so many times—until she'd had no choice but to believe it—that having use of all senses wasn't a requirement for happiness. Perhaps it wasn't. She *had* found happiness in her life after the accident. But it was nothing compared to this sensory feast. The sound of Lauren's and her own breath blending in her ears. The smell of Lauren's arousal teasing her nostrils. Erica's hands firmly planted on her lover's knees, holding them apart although that wasn't necessary anymore. She'd taste her soon enough—as she had done many times before—but first, she had to look a while longer.

Lauren found Erica's hand with hers. Not to urge her to take action, Erica was sure of that, but to enjoy this moment together. There would only ever be a first of this. If Erica were to go blind again tomorrow, she wanted this view etched into her memory—along with an image of Lauren's smile, and her body standing naked in front of her.

Neither one of them seemed to have the nerve to crack a joke at this point. Nor did Erica have the time or the inclination to consider the visible changes to her own naked body. Lauren had seen it before. It didn't matter.

As though in a trance, Erica bent and pressed a kiss to Lauren's nether lips. She inhaled deeply, but she didn't want to be between her lover's legs for this. It impaired her vision too much. She pushed Lauren's legs down and found a position next to her.

"I want to see you," Erica said. "When you come."

Lauren nodded and pulled her in for a kiss and her hand trailed down Erica's stomach. They'd often done it like this because of the aural stimulation it provided. Lauren's gasps in her ear had always been a huge turn-on for Erica. This time, it wouldn't only be Lauren's moans and groans spurring Erica on.

Erica traced a finger back to Lauren's soaked pussy lips and let it skate along the pooled wetness there. Oh, the things she wanted to do. Watch her fingers disappear in her lover's cunt as she fucked her. Take in the curve of her behind for long seconds when she spun her around. But as Lauren had said at the hospital: they had all the time in the world. And right now, lust was consuming her flesh, making her clit pound and drenching her pussy in its own juices.

Erica pushed a finger deep inside of Lauren, while gazing deep into her eyes. They narrowed a fraction as her lips parted. Erica found a rhythm, and added a second finger, before Lauren touched her thumb to Erica's clit and started strumming it.

"Oh fuck." The full sensory overload was already having spectacular effects on Erica. This wouldn't be just another climax. This would be her first climax seeing Lauren. That and the fact she was simultaneously fucking Lauren, and witnessing what that was doing to her face, drove more and more blood rushing to her clit. Her heart full of love, her eyes full of light, and her lover's cunt full of fingers. There really wasn't anything more to it for

Erica then. She gave herself up to the moment, to the heat rushing to her extremities from that one point between her legs, rolling back and forth.

"I'm close," Lauren said. "Oh god, I'm close."

"Me too," Erica grunted. And while she came, she tried as hard as she could to keep her eyes wide open.

THE TALKIES

JEREMY EDWARDS

"Oh, so this will be your first?"

Damn it. Why did *Vanity Fair*'s Anne Wilmot have to put it that way, with an *oh* and a *so*?

It had been reverberating in Flora's head for days now—not with the wasplike crackle of the Vitaphone, but with the immediate, velvety warmth of gloves nestled between fingers, or of pussy quivering on the tongue. Flora saw the writer's face re-uttering those words in her mind, the woman's narrow yet sensitive nose pointing her way, her mouth precise but gentle, her eyes always seeming to pose more than one question at a time.

"Those of us who value the true theater have been asking, since the outset, if the moving picture can begin to approach it. One thing that troubles me, as an acolyte of the Drama, is the discontinuity of film production. You're forced to stop and start constantly, Miss Garfield..."

"Please do call me Flora."

Before their inaugural interview, she'd felt no anxiety about the transition. Flora had spent three seasons on the New York stage before coming to Hollywood to make what were now called silent films. Movie directors had sometimes needed to *shush* her during takes, when her continuous unscripted narration—much of it pornographic—caused her lips to move excessively, or her co-stars to lose their composure. Talking for the camera should have been the most natural form of expression for her, more liberation than challenge.

"*You're forced to stop and start, Flora. You're fortunate if you get through three consecutive lines before the camera angle needs to be changed, or the film needs to be reloaded, or the lighting need to be altered, or the makeup needs to be refreshed. Can this ever be a genuine performance, we ask, in the sense of an artist immersing herself in the character?*"

"*I... I suppose I don't know, really. But then—well, what is a 'genuine' performance? Even on the stage, I'm pretending. I can't stop between lines, but it's still just... that is, it's just an act.*"

"*Ah, so you've read Barnizelovich.*"

"*No. I—I don't know who that is, Mrs. Wilmot.*"

Now she'd become, for the first time, self-conscious. She saw herself talking, not to the camera, but to those questioning eyes. Anne Wilmot had unsettled Flora in a way no woman ever had, even lovers.

Lovers. Pressing her ass into the cushioned support of her makeup-table stool, she imagined Anne's jacket on the dressing-room floor, Anne's blouse unbuttoned, Anne's breasts soft in the mirror, despite the harsh lighting.

No, it wasn't merely the questions but also the questioner, Flora admitted.

And she also admitted that with the second interview nearing, she didn't know whether to rejoice or panic over the anatomy of these in-depth profiles, which required so much more than the usual brief between-takes indulgence of fawning gossip columnists and bored publicity-office hacks. It was an honor to be profiled by *Vanity Fair*—it was by no means a given, even for a star of Flora Garfield's importance—and it was an undertaking that entailed real conversations, multiple conversations, hours of being studied, explored, and unraveled by young Mrs. Wilmot.

The *Mrs.* meant nothing, everybody said. "*Less* than nothing," Flora's trousered makeup woman had whispered, with a giggle and a wink and a scrape of front teeth over her bottom lip. Mary the makeup girl was an expert in all the preferences of the studio's women, and gave them bootleg liquor at half the price she charged the men.

They called Flora "daring"—well, the gossip columnists and publicists did, anyway. But when, she asked herself as she left the dressing room, had she ever felt the queasy intoxication of what that word ought to mean? Oh, she was undeniably adventurous and ambitious, unconventional and outspoken; but inside she'd always been sure of her footing.

Today was their first day actually filming with synchronized sound. They'd been out on the lot the previous week, and out on location earlier in the month, but those quick shots of the principals walking in and out of buildings or bicycling along a country road would feature music only, no dialogue.

Once on the set, the expectation that she'd spend hours waiting through the technical adjustments relaxed her. No one would be cueing her to really act for quite a while, she assumed. A sample gesture here (preferably a rude one), a turn of the head there (with tongue extended, naturally), and maybe a filthy test phrase or two could be accomplished practically in her sleep, so long as they weren't rolling.

But as the morning dragged on and she exhausted, first, the mischievous thrill of breaking her colleagues up with her naughty antics, and then the placidity of the boredom that followed, the anxiety seeped back in. She thought of the invisible, scattered masses who would be receiving her performance: it was so much harder to conceptualize them as friends than the concentrated flesh and warmth of a theater audience. Flora could *smell* a theater audience, the eager sweat of the gentlemen and, especially, the perfumed enthusiasm of the ladies.

Still, she'd entertained the absent masses countless times before, silently. Why was this so different?

The answer was obvious: it was different because, in her own voice, she now heard the vulnerable honesty of the in-depth interviewee. She heard the shaky courage of a superficial stage woman being listened to by a poised, intelligent woman of letters—a woman who sat with her slender legs crossed and a crisp notepad in her lap, a woman whose throaty eloquence sounded to Flora like a fucking session on a tea table.

Did Mr. Wilmot ever fuck her, before the divorce? Flora wondered, feeling a trickle of wetness race down the seam of her underclothing. *I could do it better, I know I could.* Her confidence surged, but it was a wild sexual confidence, not a sober artistic one. Her breathing was short, her nipples scratched deliciously but inconveniently against her camisole, and she was tempted to break her own production-day rule and order a little liquid something from Mary, just to calm herself.

No, instead she would announce loudly, though in this instance falsely, that she needed to pee. The crew always seemed to get a kick out of that, welcoming the image of their statuesque blonde star with her undies down. Then she'd take advantage of the privacy to tickle the hell out of her pussy and thereby restore her equilibrium.

She was about to stride forward, with a calculated wiggle in her step, to excuse herself to her private bathroom, when two things happened. First, the director addressed her for the first time in forty-five minutes: "Miss Garfield, I think we're ready for a take."

Second, Flora's eye was drawn to the entry door far at the rear of the soundstage, where a silent shaft of sunlight introduced a visitor onto the set. It was Anne Wilmot; her magazine had arranged for a full studio pass, of course.

"Remember, everyone, we are recording with sound. Nobody is to speak, apart from the actors reciting their dialogue, until I yell 'cut.'"

The director rattled off a few last instructions to the crew, before shouting "Action!"

"I'm surprised you came here, Melanie," Flora's tuxedoed co-star began. "True, I'd hoped we might meet again." He pronounced it *uh-gayn*, showing off his British accent, which rumor said he'd originated in his hometown of Kansas City circa 1919. "But *here? Today?*"

"It was tomorrow or never, Horace."

"Cut! Okay, Miss Garfield, the line is, 'It was today or never.'"

"Oh. No 'Horace'?"

"No, no, 'It was today or never, Horace.' *Today.* You said 'tomorrow.'"

"Hey, you're not gonna let her change what I wrote, are you, Isaac?"

"Shut up, Mr. Elwitz." Having snapped at the screenplay author, Isaac resumed speaking courteously to Flora. "Miss Garfield, 'tomorrow' doesn't make sense, you see? It has to be 'today.'"

"Of course. I'm not fucking stupid, you know. I just misspoke, that's all. I didn't even realize I'd said the wrong word. I'm sorry." The apology shot rudely up from her throat in tandem with the flush of discomfiture rising the length of her neck.

She'd said the wrong word, she realized, because that wrong word, *tomorrow*, was the day of her next interview session with Anne, and thus the day swamping her thoughts.

And it shuddered through her that *this* was the first thing Anne had seen of her performance: Flora making an ass of herself. Flora looking unprofessional. Flora speaking sharply to an ever-patient director.

The cameras rolled again, and again came her cue.

She said the line correctly this time.

"Cut! Sorry, Miss Garfield, we have to do that one more time. Bob's signaling me that the sound dropped out."

"The sound is fine, chief," Bob clarified, "but she swallowed the last part of her line. The mike hardly picked up a thing."

She knew that the bespectacled technician was correct, damn him. She'd felt it happening. In three years of theatrical work, her delivery had been impeccable, scene after scene, even when she'd been struggling through a chest cold… and now she couldn't get a one-sentence line out properly.

"This is new for all of us," Isaac said kindly. "I'm not expecting anyone to get it right the first time."

Somehow, his tolerance made her embarrassment even more onerous. Didn't he see that *she* should have done it right the first time? Had she made herself look like just another silent-screen mannequin, who had to be taught how to speak?

She turned away, desperate to compose herself—but as she did so her gaze flitted past Anne, who was now seated attentively behind all the technicians, her notebook in hand. Their eyes met, and suddenly Flora was once again reliving their recent conversation.

"In any event, one approaches closer to the ideal—I will always take the stage as the ideal, you understand—in a talking picture, no doubt. Tell me, does acting in talking pictures, in your opinion, allow you more engagement with the character, even if it can't be sustained at length?"

"I guess it might. I'll be better able to say in a few days, once I've had the experience of real talkie filming."

"Oh, so this will be your first?"

"Action!"

"I'm surprised you came here, Melanie. True, I'd hoped we might meet again. But *here? Today?*"

Her lips froze like berries caught in an early frost. *The Drama. Genuine performance. Anne Wilmot. The talkies, moving pictures with moving tongues. Hot moving tongues. The ideal. Teach me, teach me to speak. Teach me, Anne...*

Her hesitation lasted too long—and instead of delivering Melanie's answer, she heard herself scream in frustration. Feigning an attack of acute nervous nausea, she ran away to masturbate.

When she returned, Anne had gone. Flora had come fast and hard astride the toilet seat; had troubled Mary for a glass of water and a touch-up to her face; and had resolved with great self-consciousness to be un-self-conscious.

She did her job competently, though not excellently, the rest of the day, and the hungry camera was satisfied. Flora herself was anything but.

When she entered her dressing room that evening she found frisky Mary waiting, as she sometimes did, in a state of partial undress. Today she was cutely, roundly bottomless, not even quite sexy—a sliver shy of sexy, for the time being. Though her ass was emphatically bare, her workingman's cap still surmounted her bobbed haircut.

"Rough day, huh, gorgeous? I thought you might like something warm to grab ahold of." The makeup girl immediately led Flora to the daybed, and settled her nude behind onto the star's lap.

Flora kissed her appreciatively on the nose, then gave her pale pink derriere two small slaps and a squeeze. "No, not today, Mary." She rose. "But thank you, my dear."

Had she ever turned Mary down before? she caught herself wondering into the mirror. Normally, she would have been meloning her face into the woman's smiling crotch by now. It was not as if Flora didn't feel horny. On the contrary, she was once more beginning to feel aroused to an impractical degree. And yet Mary held no sexual interest for her, at this moment.

At home in her little mansion, Flora slept half the night with her fingers between her thighs, the other half with the delicate friction of a gnarled sheet pulled tightly from her buttocks cleft forward. The most vivid of the dreams had her reclining on the daybed in her dressing room, where Anne Wilmot indulged her desires, as Mary had once done for her in waking life, by tickling her through various strategically situated holes that the makeup girl had obligingly cut into a set of Flora's lingerie. The dreamland Mrs. Wilmot tickled with silky feathers and impressive verbal fanfare, and Flora said "I love you" in her sleep.

In the morning, she didn't leave her bed until she'd diddled her clit to its rightful release, her heels threatening to drill holes in the mattress. Never had she known such a feverish lust: eros had always been a hearty and frequent pleasure, but a casual one.

Afterward, she eschewed the luxury of her bathroom and danced her welling bladder into the back garden, where the walls gave her utter privacy and she could pose in her negligee to pee freely in the outdoors, as she preferred. Exhausted from her state of arousal and the exertions of addressing it, Flora squatted, roared open, and imagined she was peeing away her heated passion, so she might have a restful, serene morning before it returned.

But the cajoling slap of the breeze on her exposed bottom, the torrential intimacy of emptying, and the hot kiss of droplets along her pussy and upper thigh flesh conspired to excite Flora anew... and her untamable mind threw forth a striking picture of Anne Wilmot in a similar setting—handsome Anne Wilmot alone among the trees, lowering a pair of jodhpurs to piss like a horsewoman.

The image did not leave Flora serene.

After lunch, Anne arrived at the house for their Sunday interview session. Flora noticed she was wearing a shorter skirt this afternoon and, in an otherwise subdued ensemble, an obscenely crimson boutonniere.

The conversation took place over coffee. Anne's was laced with more than a few drops of Mary's whisky, an invitation she'd embraced when Flora had made it, though her hostess was taking hers only with cream. Perhaps, Flora thought, this would put them on more of an even footing intellectually: the sober screen girl and the tipsy critic.

Sober, though, was hardly the word, she reflected. Her pulse skittered from being with Mrs. Wilmot, and her nostrils were giddy from the tangs of feminine chemistry Flora detected each time Anne shifted or recrossed her thighs. Anne's womanhood smelled alert, and Flora's once again warmed drunkenly under her clothes.

"Since our last conversation," said Mrs. Wilmot, "I've given much thought to what you said about genuine performances. Perhaps the true artists, like you, assiduously exercise their craft—what you humbly called 'just an act'—in whatever form is required, be it the seamless, mesmerizing pageantry of the stage or the piecework of the motion-picture factory floor. Perhaps it is only we critics who worry foolishly about such things as immersion and continuity."

"I'm—I'm honored that you consider me a true artist." And, moreover, she was stunned that her clumsy, faltering speeches at the last interview could have proved meaningful to Anne.

"After all, it is why I'm here." Anne leaned forward in her chair, setting her cup and notebook aside, her eyes bright with intelligence and alcohol. "I knew your presence on the stage, Flora. Your grace, your emotional keenness, your voice overcame me. As an acolyte of the Drama. And," she added in a lower key, after a dignified pause, "as a woman."

She stood up, approaching Flora while she continued to talk. "And when I learned you were making pictures, I went to see one—though at the time I detested pictures. I went, and I watched, and I stayed and watched you again."

Anne reseated herself next to Flora on the sofa. "In the dark, seated alone in a less crowded showing, my hands went up my skirt while I watched you. And as I read the title cards I heard them in your voice, your real voice that you'd imprinted on my memory. I heard you, I watched you, I touched myself, I moistened my seat... I wept with pleasure in the two-penny midnight of the afternoon."

Flora's panties were a puddle, her breast a bonfire. She wasn't sure how to respond—she wanted to declaim sex-permeated monologues to this woman whose oratory had flowed for her, but again she was self-conscious. "You left the set quickly yesterday," was what finally came out of her mouth.

"Yes. I flattered myself that it was I who had unnerved you." Mrs. Wilmot's efficient little hand was on Flora's stocking, right where it stretched yearningly over the erogenous knob of her knee. "I apologize—it was not my intention to do so. Or, I should say, to do so at that time and in that place." She stroked the stockinged kneecap. "Maybe I should have told you at our first interview how much I... admired you. But I didn't want you to take me for a star-dazzled sycophant. I couldn't bear to let you despise me." Her fingers stroked upward, under Flora's skirt. "You don't despise me, do you, Flora?"

"Unnh," the star growled, unable to stand the tension any longer. She grasped Mrs. Wilmot's face in both her hands and sucked ravenously on her lips.

Anne clutched at Flora's haunches and pulled her

downward. The stiff fabric of Mrs. Wilmot's jacket teased Flora's tits through her cotton blouse, and the stimulation was heavenly.

But Flora had wanted Anne's bosom naked since she'd visualized it in her dressing-room mirror, and soon she was frantically exposing the woman. The jacket opened, then the blouse... and when she was confronted with the ivory-colored bodice of Anne's camiknickers, Flora used her teeth to edge the straps down enough to loosen the garment, and her hands to coax Mrs. Wilmot's small pastry breasts upward into sight. She tongued Anne's nipples; Anne closed her eyes, and her mound rubbed Flora's through the curtain of their skirts.

But the sofa was awkward, and Flora asked Anne to join her in her bedroom—where she knew the sheets held the aroma of her restless night and daybreak.

The hostess disencumbered herself from her shoes and stockings before leaving the parlor, and her guest did the same. Anne then followed Flora down the hall at a clip, the top of her undergarment still in delicious disarray, her breasts glistening where Flora's tongue had wet them.

Once gaining the bed, Mrs. Wilmot surprised Flora by lifting the star from behind and situating her, rump up, over her lap. Anne breathed with an audible intensity as she raised Flora's hem to the waist and gave her panty-clad ass a series of vigorous slap-caresses. "Oh, my beauty," Anne cooed, alto.

She tickled Flora inside her panty leg—which, as in her dream, made Flora wild with excitement—and the lovers play-wrestled themselves toward the headboard. Going between Anne's spread-eagled thighs, Flora found what she was looking for: the gape where the camiknickers were left unseamed.

Her fingers parted the fabric lips open, then did the same with the flesh they harbored. Anne's juice slickened her, and she probed further—up and down the slit, inward and outward, spreading the nectar as far as Anne's clit and her rear dimple, while her guest writhed on the bed.

Anne's underwear felt cool against Flora's cheeks when Flora went down on her, but the woman's core was hot as July. Flora feasted on it, with one hand cupping Mrs. Wilmot's ass and the other busy at home, where her own desire pulsed and squirmed. The critic bucked wantonly as the actress delighted every cranny of her cunt, and Flora's mind reeled from the consciousness, or self-consciousness, that she was fucking this exquisite intellectual's head off.

She came when Anne did, and they rolled together madly before Anne took Flora's panties down, kissed her thoroughly across her bottom, and licked her way up the star's thighs. Her tongue on Flora's honeypot seemed the most intense caress Flora had ever felt, and she could only whimper, lost in layered pleasure. This time, it was not so much that she climaxed, as that she tingled and moaned through one long orgasm, until she could stand no more joy between her legs and her receptors simply shut down, like electricity sparking out to leave Flora in the calm of candlelight. One moment she was gurgling Anne's name, in an ecstasy so thick even the single syllable slurred in her theatrically trained mouth; the next moment, all was numbness and contentment, and Anne was kissing her face all over.

When they were washed and reclothed, Flora served more coffee and insisted they resume the interview. "I know you have a deadline, and I don't want to waste your time."

Anne laughed at that. The sound of it resonated cozily in Flora's chest, and she realized she was more relaxed than she'd been in weeks.

The interviewer retrieved her notebook and

undertook her professional task.

"So then, let's further discuss talking pictures, if we might. Do you find you're excited?"

"I find, now, that I am, Mrs. Wilmot." She stared unflinchingly at the writer's fascinated, fascinating face. "As you know, this is my first."

BEFORE THE BUS COMES
TAMSIN FLOWERS

If you were to die unexpectedly, tomorrow say, under the wheels of a bus, what would be your biggest regret? The one thing you did that you wish you hadn't? Or perhaps the bucket list fantasy you never got around to doing? Think about it. And then go and deal with it. Because you never know what's coming, just around the corner.

I was out for a drink with my girlfriends, Casey and Blonde, when the subject came up. We three, all the wrong side of thirty, all recently divested of our long-term significant others, liked to exercise our jaws on a Tuesday night, while lubricating our throats with a pitcher or two of Bloody Mary.

"What would you do if you died tomorrow?" said Casey. She signaled to the boy behind the bar for another jug.

"Nothing," I said. "I'd be dead."

"Yeah, Red's dead," said Blonde, with an explosive giggle; we were already one jug down.

I'm gonna take a moment to explain: yes, my hair is red, which is why my friends call me Red, but Blonde is a brunette called Sheila. We thought it funny in high school to shorten her family name—Blondell—to Blonde, and it stuck.

"I mean," said Casey, folding her arms, "if you were going to die tomorrow, what would you do tonight?"

"One last fantasy to tick off the list?" I said.

"Easy," said Blonde. "Not what, who? Chris

Hemsworth, hold on to your pants!'"

So then we were onto the-wonder-of-Chris-Hemsworth conversation, which suited me fine. Because, truth be told, I didn't want to admit to my two closest girlfriends what I would regret if I died tomorrow.

My biggest regret? Easy: I'd never slept with a woman.

I thought about it more when I got home later. Thirty-four years old, fresh out of a five-year relationship with a man whom I thought I'd grow old with, and now I was jonesing for girl-flesh. Casey and Blonde would have been shocked if I'd admitted it. They like to drink and they like their men, but when it comes to anything else, I think they're a little buttoned up. Which is fine, and I love 'em. But I wasn't going to freak them out by telling them that rather than fucking Chris Hemsworth, I'd like to spend my last night on earth with my face buried between a beautiful girl's thighs...

I think. Because that was the point. I'd never done it before and if I got knocked over the following day by the proverbial bus, I would never get the chance. Over the next few days, I thought about it more. In fact, I couldn't stop thinking about it. And everywhere I went, I kept seeing girls who looked right, like they could be the one. A cute Asian girl in Starbucks. A cool boy of a girl on the subway. A cheerleader with rock-hard abs—for god's sake! I'm not too proud to leer.

But I needed to act on this pent-up lust. I made the decision to do something, and then I sat on it for a time. A long while, in fact, each day hoping that bus wasn't due. Because I wasn't sure how to go about getting what I wanted. I've got to say here, I'm no slouch at getting people into my bed. Guys, that is. I had plenty of boyfriends throughout college, and even when I was going steady, there were plenty of times when I could have strayed if I'd wanted. But doing the whole thing in reverse, so to speak, with a girl? I didn't know where to start.

First off, how would I know whether a girl I found hot felt the same way about me? Or women at all? And would the flirting be the same?

Enough. Go to a bar. Buy a drink and see what happens.

So I did just that. Vera's had a write up as the hottest lesbian bar in my part of the city and it was big and busy, so I picked a Friday night, and headed over. No pressure—just have a drink and a look around. See if I could do this thing, scratch this itch.

That's not to say I wasn't nervous. I walked past Vera's twice with shaking hands and a tight ball of anxiety pushing at the base of my throat. But then I saw three girls come tumbling out, giggling and clutching one another's arms, and they could have been Casey, Blonde, and me. So I took a deep breath, and as a crowded bus sped past blaring its horn at a jaywalker, I pushed open the door of the bar and stepped inside.

At this point, you want me to say I stepped into another world and my life changed for good. But, no, it really looked like any other bar, and the clientele, apart from the fact there were virtually no guys, looked the same as in any other bar. Rock music blasted out and sweaty bodies heaved to the beat on a tiny dance floor. I had to elbow my way to the bar, and I don't know whether I trod on more toes than trod on mine. But I liked it—the air smelled sexy with the collective fug of hot girls having fun.

I ordered a beer, feeling pleased with myself. Such bravery! And for once I had dressed right—skinny jeans, band t-shirt, and badass boots. I was rocking it and ready to rock it with someone else. Or I would be after I'd downed a couple of beers to blow away my inhibitions. But I was in no hurry. I wanted to slip into this easily, slowly...

I saw her almost straight away. After the second sip of beer, my attention was snagged by a petite girl at the other end of the bar. Not a ravishing beauty, but she had the sort of retroussé nose I'd obsessed about through high school, and her dirty blond hair was pulled up into a scruffy pony tail from which plenty had escaped. Her wide-set dark eyes were fixed on the girl behind the bar and I instantly wished they were looking at me.

I watched her order with a small, round mouth and then she fidgeted while she waited for two beers to be drawn. Damn! She was with someone. I was starting to feel distinctly masculine in my behavior—check out the hot girl, assess your chances... Something about her got to me and I was horny as hell.

Now, shit, what was the etiquette for chatting up a girl who might be here with her girlfriend or who might just be here with a friend? I drank my beer and watched her making slow progress through the crush around the bar. Her skimpy tank showed off well-muscled arms and shoulders and, when I caught a glimpse of how tight her jeans were, I wanted to see more. I had come here to enjoy myself but I wondered if I'd leave feeling tortured instead. Maybe I should just go home and play with the rabbit.

No. I'd come here with a purpose and the rabbit could fuck itself. I finished my drink and settled on the time-tested classic approach—bump into the girl and spill her beer. Offer to replace spilled drink. Hang around chatting until she blows me off, one way or another.

In my imagination, she'd bought the other beer for me, would emerge from the crowd, and hand it to me with a smile and a knowing wink. But in actual fact, I'd lost her in the throng and she wouldn't have even noticed me anyway. I needed to cruise the room for her under the pretence of heading back to the bar. And that was no hardship, pushing my way through a hundred girls who smelled enticingly of scent, sweat, and sex, and favored tight, tight clothing.

Oops!

The fact that I did actually accidentally bump into my girl and spill her beer, rather than pretending to, I took to be a good sign. But she evidently didn't as she looked down at her beer-spattered leg.

"Sonofabitch!"

Up close, she was even prettier and my heart started flailing in my chest. An anxiety attack. Great!

She stared at me with her dark eyes and, instead of saying sorry, I remained mute. The-cat-got-my-tongue big time. Her eyes narrowed.

"You did that on purpose, didn't you?" she said.

I shook my head frantically.

"Yes, you did," she said, nodding slowly. "I saw you checking me out earlier. Fuck you!"

"Let me get you another beer," I said.

"Forget it. Hardly any spilled."

She stared at me. I looked down at the beers in her hands. She was right. One glass had an inch less beer than the other but that was all.

And then she smiled and it really did things to me. Deep down inside things.

"Here," she said, and held out the beer I'd jogged.

"What about...? Didn't you buy this for someone?"

"Just a girl," she said with a shrug of one shoulder. "She wasn't as cute as you."

You know. That moment when your heart does a flick-flack. But it felt weird to be called cute by a girl six inches shorter and, I'd guess, five years younger. Was it somehow obvious I was a newbie to the scene? I didn't know how to respond to this so I drank beer, a bit too fast.

She watched me over the rim of her glass and

downed her beer in one.

"Dance?"

I finished off my beer.

"Yeah."

She grabbed my empty glass and dumped it on a nearby table. Then she pulled me through the bodies toward the dance floor. It was the size of a postage stamp and the grinding, writhing mass of dancers, rolling their hips in time to the thumping bass line, spilled over on all sides, practically indistinguishable from the non-dancers and drinkers surrounding it . We made our way to the center of the floor, where there was only enough space to dance real close to your partner, and everyone else besides.

It was hot and she was hot. I was hot. Okay, it sounds like the chorus of a bad pop song but if nothing else had happened that evening, I would have gone home happy. I love dancing, but I couldn't remember the last time I did—and, well, this time I was dancing with a girl I wanted to fuck. She brushed against me and I brushed right back and each time it sent a little shiver of current up my spine and down to my belly. I knew it had the same effect on her when I saw a rash of goose bumps puckering the skin on her arms. There was no way she felt cold, and my forearm had just nudged the side of her breast.

She smiled at me, and I let my gaze drop. Her nipples were hard and clearly visible through the fabric of her top. I wanted to touch them and my mouth went dry. My heart was competing with the thud-thud-thud of the drum track. I hooked the back of her neck with my arm to draw her closer.

"Can we get out of here?" I said, ramping my volume so she could hear me over the music.

She nodded and raised both her hands up to either side of my face, pulling my head down. I'd be lying if I said, at this point, I wasn't terrified. I'd never kissed a woman before and I wanted to like it. But what if I didn't? I didn't have time to answer that. Her lips were on mine and not with the feminine, tentative kiss I was expecting. They were hungry and moved across mine as if they owned them, as if they'd been there before. She held my head steady and caught my lower lip in her teeth, pulling it down, tugging it sideways.

I stopped dancing and linked my arms behind her waist. I didn't care that we were in the middle of the dance floor, in front of everybody. The old me would never have behaved like this but now I threw caution to the wind and I kissed her back, staking my ownership of her mouth just as forcefully. Our tongues met and passed against each other as we both explored. Her mouth tasted of beer, slightly sweet, but fresh. I wanted the kiss to last for a long time and I was happy when it did.

The music tempo changed to Hi-NRG and she broke away abruptly.

"Come on," she said, weaving through the mass of bodies.

I followed her outside and once we were on the street, she pushed me up against the wall. She put her hands on my shoulders and I swear she was standing on her toes to even out the height difference. Her face came toward mine and I thought she was going to kiss me again. But she didn't. She brought her lips up close to my ear.

"I want to fuck you," she said, so only I could hear, although there were plenty of people going by. "Come home with me."

Words failed me but I nodded. Maybe I appeared cool and calm, but on the inside my guts were churning. Wow! This thing was really going to happen. I'd imagined it so many times, with so many different girls, but this was the one, so I plundered her mouth with another kiss.

Her top lip tasted salty and her tank clung to her, damp with sweat. Nothing had ever seemed so sexy to me as the musky smell of this girl hot off the dance floor and I didn't know if I could even wait to get back to her place. God, I hoped she lived close by.

We headed to the subway and kissed again at the dark end of the platform. When there were too many people in the car for us to carry on, I twisted one of her fingers with mine and asked her name.

"Lara," she said. "Yours?"

Who was I? Not my usual self, not Red, so I told her my given name.

"Phylicia."

She raised an eyebrow.

"I'll call you Red."

Perhaps I was my usual self, after all. But if Lara wondered why I smiled, she didn't ask.

Her apartment was a small walk-up in a rundown block a couple of minutes from the subway. She took my hand as we climbed the stairs and didn't let go even as she fumbled in her pocket for her keys. Once we were inside, we were two gone girls. She didn't offer me a drink. I didn't want one. She didn't even put on the lights. As soon as the front door closed behind us, she was pulling up my t-shirt and searching out the button at the top of my jeans.

The front door opened straight into the living room but it was too dark to see the apartment and I didn't care. I was discovering a new world underneath Lara's clothes. I peeled off her tank and her jeans, leaving her standing before me in just her panties. She had me naked, and her hands roamed freely over my back, torso and chest and, even though I wanted her to stay still for a moment so I could just look at her, I wanted to feel her touch on my body even more.

With her hands on my waist, she steered me toward

an armchair on the far side of the room. She pushed me down onto it and kneeled in front of me. Her hands separated my legs, and with a sharp intake of breath, I let her. Her palms slid up my inner thighs, coming to rest lightly on the junction between them and what lay between. She peered at me in the darkness, at my cunt, and I heard her draw a deep breath to catch the smell of me.

"Can I put a light on?" she said.

Her voice was low and throaty. She sounded as turned on as I was.

"Sure."

She got up and turned on a small table lamp a few feet away. The armchair fell within its pool of warm, golden light; the rest of the room remained dark. She came back to me with a smile on her face and dropped to the floor again.

"God, look at you," she said. "A true redhead."

She giggled and I was pleased I was freshly waxed with only a neat, narrow strip pointing the way further down.

"I've been hungry for this since you spilled beer on me."

I slid my hips forward in the chair and spread my legs wider. She reached up with one hand and touched me, running the tip of a finger along the center of my slit, so softly I hardly knew it was there. But I did know, and it made me whimper. I wanted to feel her push the finger deeper between my lips, up into my cunt, and run it up and down, and search out my most sensitive spot.

She did all that and more. When she'd explored thoroughly with her fingers, she brought her mouth in close and blew softly across my pussy. For a second she paused, as if momentarily unsure. Then warm air gave way to the wet sweep of her tongue, up and down the cleft between my lips, tracing a path up to and around my clit, interspersed with small nips of her teeth. Within a few seconds, she had to grab my hips and push me back against the chair to stop me bucking, but it felt good to fight against her and I pushed back with legs braced against the floor.

She sucked my clit into her mouth, pulling it with her lips, catching it between her teeth. I knew I was making a noise but I didn't care. She sucked hard and my back arched until I thought it would break. Every muscle deep inside contracted as I came, long and loud. My hands grabbed her hair, desperate to keep her mouth on my cunt, but she wasn't going anywhere anyway. She kept working my clit until I'd writhed right over the edge of the chair and we both sank awkwardly to the floor. She kept at it until I didn't know where I was or even who I was. And she kept going until finally I had to push her away because I couldn't take it anymore.

I lay panting on my back, legs still splayed, reveling in the touch of the cool night air on my hot, wet thighs. Lara lay on her side next to me, her body pressed up against mine, one finger idly tracing a circle around one of my breasts. I thought I was spent but my nipple perked up and my body turned toward hers without any thought on my part.

"Lara..."

I liked the sound of her name on my tongue. I liked the heat of her skin under my fingers. She had small, firm breasts, just a perfect mouthful on each side, and as I sucked one of her nipples into my mouth, I felt the familiar rush of heat between my legs. It was different to being with a man but my response was just as intense, just as fast, and just as pleasurable. Correction. When one of her hands slid down between my legs and reignited the firestorm... More intense. More pleasurable.

I kissed her on the mouth and then I pushed her onto her back and slipped my way down her body, tracing the soft contours of her belly and the hard jut of her hipbones with my fingers and my lips in tandem until she writhed underneath me. Her little moans, forcing an escape as she bit her lips against them, turned me on even more, and as my mouth smoothed its way south from her navel, I stretched one hand up to twist her nipple, making her moan much louder.

I yanked off her panties and threw them aside. Her splayed legs were facing away from our little pool of light but I didn't mind. I wanted to explore her in the dark, to feel and touch and taste her treasures without seeing them. I slipped my hand over her mound and took the plunge to where her flesh was softest, moist with sweat and juices, where I knew she was aching to be touched.

I pushed two fingers up inside her and then—and this was the moment for me, what this whole thing was about—I kissed her pussy. I was tentative at first, just darting with my tongue, soft touches with my lips. But the salty taste and her appreciative noises soon made me bold. I swept my tongue up her central groove until I felt the firm budding flesh of her clit. Her thighs jerked as I brought my tongue over it in a long sweep and, when I circled it, she raised her hips up off the floor to give me more.

I took what she offered. I pulled and bit and sucked, and all the while fucked her hard with my fingers. I couldn't get enough and I was a greedy child, slurping away, with my free hand working first one breast, then the other. She twisted underneath me at every touch and her body became as drenched with sweat as my face was with her juices. She tasted so good and when finally I took my hand away from her breasts to reach down to my own clit, we both came, she with a shriek of pleasure, I with a low groan which built in volume as my climax climbed within me.

I slept there, on the floor, and I think Lara did too,

though when I woke someone had put a pillow under my head and a quilt stretched across both our bodies. It was still dark and I felt stiff and cold where I lay but I didn't dare move lest I disturb her. She had one arm flung across my chest, her hand lightly resting on my nipple. I smiled, happy to wait.

Eventually, as the darkness turned to gray, she stirred. Her head went to my chest and she latched onto one breast with her mouth. I stroked her hair and she looked up at me. She reached a finger up and pushed it into my mouth. I bit down playfully.

"Lara," I said, "I have a confession."

She let go of my breast with her mouth and rolled on top of me so we were chest-to-chest, face-to-face.

"What?"

"That was the first time for me. I'd never slept with a woman before."

I don't know why I felt it important to tell her this. It just was. But she laughed, not the reaction I expected.

"And?" I said, frowning.

"Me too," she said.

What the fuck?

"You're my first girl," she said.

"D'you think we did it right?" I said, though I knew damn well she'd done it right for me.

"So fucking right."

"Would you do it again?"

"Try and stop me."

"Now?"

Her grin became roguish and she disappeared under the quilt.

I lay back, letting my legs go slack and wide as a frisson of excitement tightened my belly. I felt Lara's hand start its exploration.

I'm ready to be run over by that bus. But I still hope it's a long time coming.

WHOLE AGAIN
BRENDA MURPHY

"Ray, if you sing that song one more time, I swear I'm going to hit you with this frying pan." I turned back to the stove. Forever stuck in the sixties, Ray thought singing "Brown Sugar" at me was hilarious.

"Geez, don't be so sensitive," he said. Shoes squeaking, Ray crossed the greasy kitchen floor and went to the back to yell at the kid he'd hired to wash dishes. The kid spent most of his time getting stoned in the walk-in when Ray wasn't around. Tuning out Ray's yelling, I turned out the special I was frying and plated it. I slid it along the steel counter, slapped the bell, and spun the rack. Ten more tickets were hanging.

I could see part of the house through the pass. Another Thursday night with old ladies in print dresses, old men in sharp creased shirts, thirty-somethings trying to eat while peeling their kids off the ceiling, and the loners at the counter. Nobody really cared about what they were eating as long as it came to the table hot, fried, salty, and a lot of it. I plowed through the orders. Most of the waitresses were lifers, the kind of ladies that had been working there so long they seemed part of the furniture. Too broke to retire, most of them would work until the trays were too heavy, or they forgot orders. All of them were old enough to have birthed me; most of them were glad they hadn't. Ray was so short of cooks when I applied, he didn't care about my skills or my face.

"A Vet, huh? I get credit for hiring Vets," he had

53

said rubbing his hand across the stubble on his chin. Some guys looked fashionable in stubble; Ray looked like he'd lost his razor.

"Can you start tonight?" he had asked, shuffling through papers that overflowed his desk and covered the floor of his office.

"Sure," I had said, happy that I wasn't going to have to sit alone in my mom's empty house, dark and cold, because the electric was off and I didn't have enough cash to have it turned back on. I quit gathering wool and went back to work, knowing that if I slowed down I'd get buried. Ray had promised to hire another cook, but it had been two years now and he hadn't made good on it. I focused on cooking, praying that nobody had a special order.

"Hey Cookie!" Sally, the head waitress, never called me by my name, she just called me what she called every other cook she had ever worked with at the diner.

"I need some fries on a rail. Jesus, that new girl is in the weeds. I don't know why Ray hired her."

Sliding the hot fries to Sally I looked past her at the new girl. I knew why Ray had hired her. I would have too. Bent over a four top, her uniform was stretched just tight enough to show off her assets, which were considerable. When she straightened and turned to walk to the pass, the view was even better.

"Hey, Hon, your tongue is hanging out," Sally said, as she hurried away with the fries. The new girl arrived at the pass, order slip fluttering in her hand. Short auburn hair framed her face. The clip was hard to open and she swore when she snapped a nail.

"Don't try so hard," I said, hoping I sounded helpful, and not like an ass. She looked up, caught sight of my face, and looked down.

"What?" she said

I took the slip from her hand. "You have to slide it

in, easy, like this." I slipped the order under the clip. Now I hoped I didn't sound creepy.

"Thanks," she said spinning away from me and hurrying to her tables.

"And hit the bell," I called to her, slapping the bell. I went back to my station. The orders kept rolling until we closed. Finally, the last order was plated and I shut down the grill. My legs were killing me, even the one that wasn't there. The stoned kid was singing his ass off washing dishes. Vacuums hummed as the waitresses cleaned up the front of the house. Wiping down my station, I imagined what it would be like to cook in a restaurant where people judged your cooking by how it tasted, not how large the portion was, or how fast you cooked it.

I walked back to the staff room and tossed my apron in the laundry. There was a tap at my shoulder, and I turned around, expecting Ray to be there reminding me not to take so much time to make my dishes look good. It was the new girl, standing close, twisting her apron in her hands.

"Hey, I didn't say thank you for helping me. I'm Kate." Her apron hit the hamper, and she stuck out her hand. I took it, liking the feel of her soft fingers, and firm grip.

"I'm Jennifer, my friends call me Jay," I said, holding her hand as long as I dared.

"I'm new."

"I noticed," I said. She laughed. Small lines etched the corners of her pale green eyes. Her laugh was rich and full of round notes. I wanted to hear it again.

"Do you want to get something to drink?" The words came out of my mouth before I could stop them.

"Well, um." She shifted her eyes, avoiding mine. Sally must have tipped her off. In my head, I could hear her laying it out for Kate in her two-pack-a-day rasp.

"Cookie's a dyke, Ray's a creep, the dishwasher is a stoner, lock your purse in your locker, carry extra sugar and ketchup in your apron, and fold the napkins so they make a pocket for the silverware."

"Never mind. I understand." I pushed past before she had time to come up with some phony excuse for why she couldn't be seen with me.

* * *

I glanced in the rearview mirror as I pulled out of the parking lot. Kate was heading for the bus stop. I pulled over once I was around the corner. I wanted to keep driving, to pretend that it didn't matter, that I didn't care, that I would be able to forget about her laugh, and how her eyes crinkled at the corners when she smiled. I wanted to pretend that I would go home to an empty house and be fine with it. I wanted to, but I couldn't. I sighed, watching the bus stop in my rearview. Watching as she twisted the handle of her purse slung over her shoulder, watching as she started to sit on the bench crusted with snot and gum and thought better of it. Watching and wanting and cursing myself for sitting there watching her instead of offering her a ride.

"Fuck it," I said banging my hand on the wheel. I reversed fast, coming to a halt at the bus stop. She backed up to the far wall of the bus shelter. I rolled the passenger window down and leaned over.

"Hey, it's Jay, from the diner. You want a ride home?"

"You mean instead of waiting in this creepy bus stop? Hell yeah."

I popped the lock and she climbed in. "If you're going to let me drive you home, why did you turn me down before?"

"You asked if I wanted to get something to drink. That's different." The bus pulled up behind me, horn blaring and I pulled out of the bus lane.

"Where's home?"

"Fifteen forty-one South Street," she said, settling into the seat.

I was feeling bold for the first time in forever as I looked over at her, liking the way her skirt hiked up just a little when she sat back, showing off her thighs. Loving that she didn't bother to tug it down.

"You sure you don't want to go for a drink?" I said.

"Look, I just spent ten hours serving incredibly craptastic food to a bunch of people that don't tip worth a damn. My feet hurt, my hair stinks like grease, and I cannot wait to get out of this uniform. I just want to go home."

"Craptastic?" I said.

"Shit, I'm sorry. I forgot."

I shook my head. "No, you're right, it is craptastic. I hate cooking it, but the people who eat at Ray's just care about the portions."

"Have you worked there long?" she asked.

"Two years. My mom wanted me to come home so she could help me, after my time in rehab. I ended up taking care of her. She passed two years ago."

"Rehab? Alcohol or drugs?"

"Leg," I said, knocking on my left leg for emphasis.

"Oh. Sorry, guess I shouldn't assume. Why did you stay?"

"I was broke. Still am. Ray was willing to give me a job. What are you doing here?" I asked.

Her voice was a whisper and she spoke to the window. "Ran out of money and luck." She twisted the handle of her purse.

I pulled up in front of a low bungalow on a side street with a shaggy yard.

She touched my arm. "Hey, I feel pretty bad about my craptastic comment. You want to come in for a drink? I'm too wired to sleep."

"I'd like that." I walked behind her, digging my nails into my palm, pushing down the hope and desire in my belly. I reminded myself it was just a drink. She turned the key in the lock, pushing the door wide. I stood in the darkness waiting for her to turn on a light. She switched on a small lamp.

"Beer?" she asked, kicking off her shoes.

"Yeah, whatever you have." She disappeared into the darkness. The living room was empty except for an old wooden card table, two light blue folding chairs, and books. Books stacked everywhere, piles spilling into each other. I checked the titles in the dim light as I made my way to a chair and sat.

Kate came out carrying two bottles of pale ale in one hand. She handed one to me and tipped her bottle taking a long swallow. I watched her as she drank, wanting to kiss my way from the bottom of her neck to her full mouth. She lowered the bottle, setting it on the table. I took a sip, letting the bitter taste of the beer roll over my tongue. Her eyes met mine. I tried to hide the hunger in my eyes, but her frown told me she had seen it. I braced myself for the "I'm not that way" talk. She leaned over me, and her hand brushed the scar on my forehead that started in my hairline. I trembled at the sensation.

"Look," she said, eyes pinning me in my chair, "if you are just playing with me, you need to leave now."

"What does that mean?" I shifted in my chair to meet her eyes.

"It means if you are a half-assed, wanna-be dyke, chubby chaser you need to get out now. I am not the new ride in town."

I raised my hands in surrender. "Hold on. You're not straight? Why did you blow me off until I offered you a ride home?"

"Because I have had my fill of curious straight girls

and dykes who think that just because I'm a big girl I will be grateful for their attention. I just want to be with someone who knows who and what they are."

"Well, how do I know you're not just some freak who feels like they need to do a gimp a favor? Or maybe just curious? Hell, I'm not a gold star lesbian, but I do know who I am. And I know what I like." I slid my hands up her full hips, and pulled her into a kiss. She leaned into me, the chair protested with a loud squeak. She pulled back.

"You sure don't kiss like a straight girl," she said.

I laughed. "Because I'm not. I can't believe Sally didn't tell you about me."

"Oh, she told me about you, and everyone else. She is homophobic and racist as hell, like most people in this damn town." Kate took another sip of her beer.

"You get used to it," I lied.

Kate tipped my head back, running her fingers through my cropped hair. I shivered, relishing her touch, leaning my head into her hand. "I like you," she said. I let her words roll over me, savoring them and her husky voice. She scooted her chair closer and sat, knees brushing against mine.

"Let me cook for you," I said.

"Why?"

"Because I haven't had anyone to cook for in a long time, because you called my cooking craptastic, and because I would like to spend more time with you when we're not tired and sweaty and burnt-out from work."

"Deal. But don't think a good meal will get you in my pants, you're going have to work for that."

I felt the heat in my face, knew my cheeks were glowing. How long had it been since I had felt like this? I couldn't remember. Before the Army, I did this type of thing all the time: banter, flirt, kiss, make plans, trust that tomorrow would come. After my tour, after my world exploded, after I came home in pieces, I had stopped. Even now I didn't speak, knowing that if I spoke she would hear every bit of desire in my voice. I finished my beer to buy time before I finally trusted myself to speak. "How about Sunday? I could make you dinner. Six okay?"

"Sunday at six works."

She walked me to the door. As I turned to leave, she spun me around and kissed me, her lips soft and full of promises that I hoped she would keep.

* * *

Ray passed by my station, his aftershave overpowering the onion I was chopping. "Jesus, Ray, what the hell do you have on?" I wiped at the air with my side towel.

"Sally got it for me for Christmas. You like it?" He swiped his hand through his hair, extra shiny with hair gel. Instead of his normal five o'clock scruff, his face was pink from a fresh shave. He was wearing gray pants and a black shirt, set off with his signature white belt and white shoes. For a Friday, Ray had gone all out.

"What's up, Ray?" I asked, grabbing another onion.

"Me." He chuckled at his own joke. "Well, I will be in a few hours. I'm taking the new girl home."

"What?" My stomach tightened.

"Yeah, I'm driving her home."

"You think that's your ticket to paradise, a ride home?" I brought the knife down hard, splitting the onion in half.

"What would you know about it? You haven't been with anyone since you came home. All you do is sit in that empty house feeling sorry for yourself. Me, I got needs. Tonight I'm going to take care of them." Taking a deep breath, I shook my head trying to erase images of Ray attempting his smarmy version of suave with Kate. I was sure Kate could handle him. I had no right to be angry, but that didn't mean I wasn't. Why the hell was she riding with him? I focused on the onion, turning it into fine dice. Ray strutted off, shoes squeaking, to the loading dock to check on the meat delivery.

* * *

"Hey gorgeous." I looked up. Kate was early. I had spent the afternoon thinking about my conversation with Ray. What did I know about Kate? One kiss, an agreement to come to my house, some flirting—maybe she was just covering all her bases.

"Hey, you getting a ride home with Ray?"

"Maybe. You got a problem with that?" She moved closer, leaning her hip against my station. Her hair was damp. She smelled like fresh lemons, tart and clean. I looked down at my hands. God, I just wanted to feel her lips again.

"No, I just…" I stopped, not knowing what to say that didn't sound like a crazy jealous stalker.

"Just what? Worried that I'm a slut? That I didn't mean it? That I'm not really queer? That I'm just another fat girl who can't turn down attention?" Her voice boomed off the tiles in the empty kitchen. I looked into her pale green eyes. Her lush lips were so close.

"No. No. I just—" I kissed her then, pulling her into me, kissing her hard, loving the feel of her soft curves in my hands. She leaned into my kiss, her hands on my back. I groaned, grinding myself into her hips, feeling the heat in my core. I ran my hands over her breasts, soft and heavy. She kissed and sucked at my lips, tugging my lower lip with her teeth. She clung to me, sliding her hands under my apron. My knees gave a little as she unzipped my pants. I gasped as she pressed on, pushing my underwear aside. I pulled back to look in her eyes, a soft green now.

"This is the answer to your question." She brought me off quick, the waves of pleasure washing over me. So long. It had been so long. I wanted to make it last, but I came hard and fast. I heard the back door open as I finished. I stumbled back, snatching my apron down and smoothing it. Kate leaned against my station. Smiling, she brought her hand up to her mouth, her tongue flicking between her fingers. I heard Ray's shoes on the floor.

"Hey, Kate." She turned to face Ray. I stepped back.

"Hey, Ray."

"We still on for tonight?" His voice cracking, Ray rocked on his toes.

I held my breath, willing myself to be cool. I wiped down my already clean station.

"No Ray, I forgot I already had a ride home. Thank you for the offer."

Ray's eyebrows lowered, his face skewed by the smile he forced. "Well, okay then. Some other time." He spun on his heel and made his way out of the kitchen to his office. I heard the soft click as he locked the door.

Kate looked at me over her shoulder, lipstick smudged, half a smile on her lips, and raised an eyebrow. "You are taking me home, right?"

* * *

"You seen Ray?" Sally asked.

"Office," I said. Sally stalked off. Ray usually worked the front of the house on the weekends, shaking hands, making a fuss over babies, and running the cash register. Sally went back to the front, grumbling. Five minutes before opening, Ray stumbled out of his office. He made his way to my station, careening between the wall and the grill. Gripping the edges of my station to steady himself, he belched. His breath reeked of cigars and the cheap scotch he kept in his desk.

"You okay?" I asked.

"You're fired," he said, jabbing a finger at me.

"What?"

"You. Are. Fired. You fucking one-legged, two-tone

dyke. Get out. Take your fat-ass girlfriend with you." He swayed as he talked. It was probably wrong to punch a drunk, but I did. Ray landed on his ass, tried to get up, and sagged back down, wiping blood off his lip. I stepped over him, ripping my apron off and tossing it to him as I did. I looked up to see the waitresses filling the pass, watching. Sally snorted and turned away. Kate's eyes met mine.

"You need a ride?" I asked.

She tossed her order pad on the counter, stripped off her apron, balled it up, and threw it at Ray's head. I bolted out the back door as if the floor was on fire. Kate caught up to me in the parking lot.

"Hey, you hit like a girl," she said as she reached out and took my hand, kissing the broken skin over my knuckles. Her laughter filled the parking lot. I found myself smiling.

"How can you laugh at what he said?" I was still shaking. She reached up, touching my cheek, wiping at the wetness there.

"Because of the look on his face when you hit him and he landed on his ass, and because he just fired his only cook and tomorrow is Valentine's Day." She started laughing again. I laughed too.

She wrapped her arms around me. "You want to drive your fat-ass girlfriend home?"

"You hungry?"

"Maybe. Or maybe I just want you to finish what I started in the kitchen."

* * *

We stood on the porch of the house that I still didn't think of as mine. She pushed up against me, grabbing my hips, grinding against me, giggling into my neck as I fumbled with the lock. Finally, I got the door open. I led her to the kitchen and opened the refrigerator. She raised her eyebrow.

"What?"

"Not the room I want to see," she said, turning and unbuttoning her blouse as she walked out.

I grabbed a bottle of cheap wine out of the fridge, kicked the door closed, and hurried after her. A bra lay in the hallway, and I followed the trail of clothes until I found her in my room, her body draped over my bed. I unscrewed the bottle top, took a long pull on the wine, and handed it to her. She brought the bottle to her lips, touching the rim with her tongue.

"You have too many clothes on," Kate said, before taking a sip of wine.

My shirt ripped as I pulled it over my head and tossed it in the corner. My nerve left me when I got to my belt buckle.

"You stopped," she said.

I looked up, blinking back tears from the edges of my eyes.

"I haven't... I mean since... my leg..." The tears started then and I had no words.

Kate slid over to the edge the bed. Gently, she took my hands in hers, and she kissed my face, kissing away my fears.

"May I?" she asked as she moved her hands to my buckle.

I nodded.

She undid my buckle with soft hands and unfastened my jeans. My heart pounded, as she slid them down. She kneeled in front of me and ran her hands over my thighs stopping at my prosthesis.

"Does it hurt?" she asked.

"No. Well, sometimes, after a long shift," I said.

She held me steady and with her help I stepped out of my jeans. She pulled me onto the bed. Looking for some liquid courage, I leaned over her, grabbing the bottle. I took another swig of the wine.

"You don't need that," she said, taking the wine from my hand and placing the bottle on the nightstand.

Her nails grazed my skin as she trailed lines up my back. I trembled as I lowered myself, sinking into her warmth. I slid my thigh between her legs, rocking into her, kissing her neck. Delighting in the feel of her skin, savoring her soft groans, and the way her body welcomed me, I trailed my hand down her belly and slipped my fingers into her wetness. Feeling powerful and strong, aching with desire, I took my time, finding myself in Kate's passion and fierce kisses.

"Please," she said. Her breath came in sighs and hisses.

My thighs were wet, slick with desire. Kate kissed me, her tongue exploring my mouth, her lips and teeth teasing me. I ground against her thigh. She slid her hand between us. I felt myself falling over the edge of pleasure and closed my eyes against it. We rocked together riding out the aftershocks. I untangled myself from her legs and sat up. She reached for the wine, took a sip, and passed it to me.

"Thank you, and I don't mean for the wine," I said.

"For what?" she said, taking the wine back.

"For not making me feel like a freak, for helping me when I needed help, and for making me laugh when I wanted to cry."

"Don't forget, I helped you get fired too." She laughed as she said it.

"I mean it. Thank you."

"I just helped you remember who you are," she said, scattering small kisses on my neck between words. I closed my eyes and focused on the soft feel of her lips, and held her close. Tomorrow would come after all.

PULLING
SACCHI GREEN

Don't look. DON'T LOOK! Keep your eyes on the horses, the judges, anything else. Anything but the bad girl of your dreams in her fuck-me-if-you-dare outfit. Look, and you'll never be able to look away.

But she was here. She'd really come. And it hadn't been just the garish lights of the midway last night; even in the noonday glare Carla smoldered, like an ember about to ignite dry leaves. The thought of stirring up that blaze made me sweat. Except it damn sure wasn't all sweat.

"She's here!" Cal said urgently. "Over by the fence!"

"Eyes front, or you're dead meat!" I snarled, just low enough not to startle the horses. The loudspeaker announcing my team drowned out my voice.

"...Ree Daniels out of Rexford, Vermont, driving Molly and Stark, with a combined weight of..."

I backed them out smoothly enough and drove briskly down the drawing ring, grip on the lines steady, attention fixed strictly on the 4200 pounds of horsepower surging ahead of me. Two great glossy black rumps pumped in unison, two muscular bodies slowed and began their turn—and Cal stumbled on my right, just managing not to drop the evener bearing half the weight of the two single-trees.

Ethan, craning to see, wavered on my left. He sped up—got into position—and the clang of the steel evener dropping onto the stone boat's hook sent the horses lurching forward with all their strength. The heavy sledge began to move. Shoulders bunched, hocks straining, hooves the size of pie plates chopping at the dirt, they pulled a load of twice their own weight across the ground, responding to my hollered commands without really needing them until the last few feet of the required distance. Training and heart were what mattered most, not driving skill, but I still wouldn't let either of my brothers handle my team in competition.

Not that Cal hadn't given it his best shot last night. "C'mon, Ree," he'd pleaded, "she said she might come on her lunch break! And I sorta let her think I'd be driving!"

"You think she cares about anything besides the bulge in your britches?" I whapped his butt right across the wallet pocket. "You can strut your studly charms all you want tomorrow night. If you get lucky enough to have a chance at slipping something inside those tight panties of hers once the midway shuts down, you can even borrow my pickup. Tonight you get to bed all sober and early and solitary, 'cause tomorrow morning your ass is mine from dawn to whenever the pull is over and the horses rubbed down and stabled."

Cal couldn't make up his mind whether to sulk or grin. He'd have looked even younger than his eighteen years if he hadn't been six-foot-six, square-jawed, and built like somebody who'd grown up tossing around fifty-pound bales of hay. My "little" brother towered over me by four inches, which still left me six-two of height and plenty of bale-tossing capacity of my own.

I almost felt guilty at letting him get his hopes up, but I sure as hell wasn't about to tell him why.

If any slipping inside Miss Carla-from-Boston's panties was going to be done, I had a bet with myself that he wasn't going to be the one doing it. Not Cal, nor any of the other young punks—and some not so young—

who hovered around her booth and pretended to be interested in throwing darts at balloons for cheesy prizes, while they watched her working her ass and tits and dark, light-my-fire eyes.

Cal and sixteen-year-old Ethan hadn't been hard to locate last night when I'd cruised the fairgrounds. Both white-blond heads, streaked hot pink and green and purple by the midway lights, loomed above the crowd. I hung back for a while near the balloon-dart booth to get an idea of what they were up to, hardly able to see the carnie huckster through the wall of testosterone-pumping adolescents between us. I could hear her slick come-on, though, and the sly, seductive tone of her voice sent hot prickles across my skin. Just food for fantasy, of course, but damn, she was good.

"C'mon folks, I'll rack 'em up again. See how Cal, here, got one right in there? Popped that cherry good? Here y'go, show us what y'got." I caught just enough movement to know she was tossing her long dark hair and twitching her hips for emphasis. "Stick that ol' dart right in! Ri-i-i-ght in there!"

"Right in where?" asked a wise guy. "Show me again!"

"If you can't find the spot on your own, hot stuff," she shot back, "maybe you better go home and practice some more on your favorite sheep."

Whoa. Considering the concentrated beer fumes in the area, she could be asking for trouble. I moved closer and squeezed in next to Cal just as the guy hurled his three darts too fast to be aiming much, and one balloon popped with a satisfying crack.

"There y'go, I knew you could hit the spot," she purred. "Prize from the first row, or wanna try again and get an upgrade?"

"How many hits to go all the way?" His leer was unmistakable.

"Sorry, Bud, my ass isn't sittin' up on the prize shelf tonight." She tossed him a big purple plush snake and moved away. "Who's next?" Her sultry gaze lit right on me, and maybe she figured it was safer not to pitch to another guy right then.

"How about you, honey? I always like to see a lady show the fellas how it's done." She put one foot up on the low barrier across the front of the booth, leaned an elbow on a sleek, black-stockinged knee and rested her chin on her hand. The top three buttons of her red satin shirt were unbuttoned, giving me a prime view of peach-tinted flesh barely held in check by a lacy black bra. Her mini-skirt was hitched up so high I caught a glimpse of matching garters and tender thighs. "How about it, darlin'?"

She sure as hell knows just how it's done! Question is, does she mean anything by it?

"Nobody here I'd call a lady," I said, looking her straight in the eye, "but I'll have a go at it anyway." I shrugged off my denim jacket and handed it to Cal, shoving him back a bit to give me room. All I wore underneath was an old white tank top smelling of sweat and horses. She handed me three darts, took my money, leaned a little farther forward, and tucked the bills loosely into her cleavage. The clueless males watching didn't seem to have any doubt that her show was for their benefit.

I raised my arm to pitch the first dart. The gaze of half the guys switched to the movement of my heavy tits—but her gaze was all that counted. And it was all I'd hoped for.

My first throw hit a red balloon, just making it bob sideways. "A real teaser, huh?" Her tone was impersonal, but a sidelong glance at my face and then my big hand hinted at more. I threw again, with a better idea of the angle required, and this time the balloon snapped and shriveled into a limp dangle of rubber. My inner tension built. When I popped the next one, too, the pressure exploding out of it seemed to pump me up right where it mattered most.

"Way to go, girl! Second shelf prize," she said. "What'll it be?"

I stifled the impulse to ask if she was still so sure her ass wasn't on that shelf. "Go on to the next guy and let me think on it a minute, okay?" I said, and she nodded, so I got down to business with my brothers. Not that I wasn't thinking on my prize real hard.

"You two go on ahead," I muttered, hauling them away. "We have to get going early tomorrow morning. Tell you what, order us all some apple crisp with ice cream down the way at that church booth, and I'll meet you there in a minute."

"Rather have some fried dough," Cal grumbled.

"Okay, whatever, anything but those damned fried onion sunburst deals!"

Cal took the money I passed him, still looking longingly back at the balloon game. Ethan looked, too, but more shyly. "Her name's Carla," Cal said. "From Boston." As if her accent, its nasal edge a notch beyond our own upcountry twangs, hadn't been a give-away. "Isn't she hot? I told her about the horse pull tomorrow, and she said she likes to watch the big ones."

"I'll bet she does," I said. "Move your butts along now." And they went. Every time they do what I say I figure it may be the last, but this time I was paying them well to help with the team, so they were less inclined to argue.

When I turned back, a girl who'd been looking for her boyfriend was making a scene at the other end of the booth. Under cover of the distraction, Carla leaned close to me. "Your brothers?" she asked, jerking her head toward Cal and Ethan's retreating asses.

"'Fraid so," I said. "You got a thing for big dumb farm boys?"

She shrugged, clearly aware that the movement made her shirt gape farther open, and that I was enjoying the view. "Not when there's a big farm girl around to distract me."

"You forgot the dumb part."

Carla looked me over slowly and thoroughly, her gaze moving down over my substantial midriff to rest on the crotch of my faded jeans.

"I'm not noticing any dumb parts," she drawled.

Damn! But attention was swinging back toward us. "So how about my prize?" I asked. "You choose for me."

She reached for a cluster of long ropes of Mardi Gras beads, slung them over my head, then swished them back and forth across my chest. My nipples responded with visible enthusiasm. "Here's a first installment," she murmured. "You gonna be around later?"

"Not tonight. Got an early wake-up call coming and a busy morning." Which wouldn't have held me back if I hadn't known Cal would come looking when I didn't show up at our RV to sleep. "Maybe tomorrow night."

"Will you be at that horse pull deal the boys were talking about?"

"Wouldn't miss it." I pulled the hank of beads off over my short pale hair and handed it back to her. "How about you hang onto these until I see you again."

A couple of customers were waving money at her by then, but Carla stuck with me for another few seconds. "Okay, but keep this one." Before I could see what she was up to my wrists were tightly bound together by a strand of purple plastic beads. "So you won't forget."

Then she was playing to the crowd of men again, hips swaying, mouth sassing. I got my own mouth closed, stepped back into the shadows, and watched for a minute. What *was* it about her? She was good-looking, but not gorgeous, and not really all that young. Which was fine with me. More than fine. What she was, was... knowing. "Hot" pretty well covered it. Hot, and on the verge of bursting into flame. Something in the way she moved, as if the stroke of her clothes along her body kept her always turned on, hinted at sexual expertise country hicks at county fairs could only imagine.

I looked down at my bound wrists and imagined plenty. Breaking the fragile string would have been easy, but I wriggled loose with care, just in time to hide the beads in my pocket before Cal and Ethan came back to find me.

My imagination kept hard at work a good part of the night, too, which might have happened even if a strand of purple beads hadn't been nestled deep into the warm, wet heat between my thighs. I wasn't a dumb farm girl, not anymore, but whatever I'd got up to with girls at UMass and then in postgrad at UConn, it hadn't been much like this. I'm not saying that no femmes go for veterinary medicine degrees, but I sure hadn't come across anybody like Carla. The way she flaunted her body, and teased mine with her eyes; the thrust of her breasts and sway of her hips, offering and daring both at the same time... Well before dawn I had to get out of the RV and find a place to do some serious solitary teasing and thrusting of my own, and even that only slowed me down to a simmer.

In the morning, the horses got me back on focus. Molly and Stark had been pulling in competitions all summer, and knew what was what. They were about as psyched up as Percherons get, and maybe more than most. The huge black horses have been bred for double-muscling for centuries, but they have spirit and heart as well.

By noon they'd come through the first few

elimination rounds and hardly broken a sweat. This last load had been more of a challenge, but they'd handled it well. There were only four teams left in competition, and two of them I knew we couldn't beat without straining hard enough to risk injury. My pair were relatively young, full-grown but without all the heft a few more years would give them, and Molly would never quite achieve the muscle mass her brother could. Letting a mare pull was, in fact, pretty rare. I got a lot of flak from old timers for it, but she had the spirit, and I'd decided to give her one more year before breeding her and complicating her life with motherhood.

I watched the loader piling another 1500 pounds of concrete blocks on the stone boat. So far I'd never set the team at a weight I wasn't sure they could handle. Should I drop out at this stage and settle for an honorable fourth? Would I quit now, if I didn't want so badly to impress somebody who was watching?

Hell no! Molly nudged me hard with her big velvety nose and blew as though in agreement. I whacked her shoulder companionably, turning my head a few degrees—and there was Carla right in my line of sight. Her mouth hung open and her eyes were wide with something that might have been fear. I grinned and nodded. Her usual cock-sure, seductive expression took over again right away, but she still eyed Molly warily.

Then Cal waved, and called to her, and I had to whack *his* shoulder to get him back on task. The first team of this round was trotting toward the loaded sledge. I was sure these huge Belgians were up to the weight, but their driver's helpers didn't get a secure hook before the horses bolted forward, and missed on the second try, too, so that by the time they did get a good hook the team was too flustered to pull together. I elbowed Cal meaningfully in the ribs.

The second team gave it a good try, but stopped a

few feet short in spite of all their driver's yelling. Then we were up. I bent for one last feel of each horse's hocks to be sure there was no tenderness, straightened from between enormous equine legs—and the quick flash of horrified awe in Carla's eyes sent a jolt of power crackling through my cunt.

Wow! But... no time for that now. No time for anything beyond keeping control of the eager horses while Cal and Ethan hustled to drop the evener onto the hook, and then the team's surge of power when I sent the order through the lines. The loaded stone boat moved, caught, moved again, slid a few feet, slowed—"Hup! Hup! Hup!" I hurled my voice at them like an extra ton of muscle, of breath, of heart, and they took it all and gave back more, struggling onward just because they refused to stop. And then the judge signaled that they'd made the distance, and the boys released the sled.

My gorgeous pair of black, sweat-flecked treasures pranced back to the far end of the arena, proud, hyped by the applause, and, I knew from their gait, just slightly sore from the strain on their hocks.

After the last team made its distance, I waved off the next round. Second place was fine for now. Molly and Stark would give me everything they had, but I didn't need to make them find their limit at the risk of injury.

When the event was over and the rosettes awarded, I drove them into the warm sunshine, keeping an eye out for Carla. Cal and Ethan had been headed off by a gaggle of cheerleader chicks, just the types that always give me flashbacks to the horrors of high school. The boys were welcome to 'em.

There she was, keeping a safe distance. "That was... something." Words uncharacteristically failed her.

"Sure was," I agreed. "I need to get them rubbed down now and tape their legs. Want to come along and make their closer acquaintance?"

"I have to get back… I'm late already… but I close down tonight at ten." Molly's inquisitive black head swung toward her. Carla stepped back in a hurry.

"Then ten is when I'll be there," I said, riding a wave of confidence.

Carla tried for a note of command. "You'd better be." She turned away, her fine ass eloquent with an assumption of power. But I'd seen some cracks in her eat-my-attitude self-possession, some fear and awe, maybe even excitement. And I'd enjoyed the hell out of how it made me feel. Those beads tight around my wrists—well, they'd sure sparked a tingle of anticipation and curiosity, and there was no denying that I'd go along with a lot just for the promise of some hot, wet, sweaty sex. Still, power was such a rush…It was going to be an interesting night, to say the least.

I was there, in fact, at eight, and again at nine, just passing by, in range of her voice but not in her line of sight. Cal caught up with me in the next row at nine thirty and groused that Carla had turned him down. "She's prowling around like a cat in heat, but says she's got other plans, and that's that. Didn't exactly tell me to fuck off, but close enough."

"You can still borrow my pickup," I said generously. "I'll probably just keep an eye on the horses tonight in the barn. What about those girls who've been trailing you around all day? I saw a couple of 'em hanging with Ethan over by the Tilt-a-Whirl." He shrugged, but grabbed my keys fast enough and took off toward the rides with a fair show of enthusiasm. Good thing he was too full of what filled his own pants to notice how his big sister was prowling around.

At ten sharp, Carla was shooing the last few customers away. I stepped up, unlatched the front canvas flap and started to lower it. "Closing time, Sport," I said to the last reluctant straggler. He started to object, tilted back his head to look up at me, paused reflexively at my chest, finally saw my expression, and decided he had business elsewhere. I dropped the flap to close us in and stepped over the low barrier, and into a role I was making up as I went along.

Her back was turned while she unclipped balloon fragments from the backboard. She'd shot me a little smile when I arrived, but there was something tentative about it, wary. Or maybe even nervous. I kind of liked the idea of making her nervous.

"So what does it take," I asked, pressing right up against her ass and putting my hands on her hips, "for a big old farm girl to distract you?"

She turned right around into my arms and did a slow grind against me. "It's been a while since I got that lucky," she said against my chin. "What do you generally have in mind when you pick up slutty carnival hucksters?"

"Once I pick 'em up," I said, digging my hands into her round asscheeks and raising her so that her breasts rested above mine, "my mind doesn't have all that much to do with it." Which was pretty much true. "But I've been known to offer to buy a girl dinner. To keep her strength up."

She grabbed onto my shoulders and pushed herself higher. My nose was right in her cleavage and her musky scent telegraphed messages all the way down to my dampening cunt. "If you're hungry," she teased, "I have better ideas. If you think you can keep your strength up."

Well, I had better ideas, too. Like digging my teeth into the lace of her bra where it peeked through her unbuttoned shirt, and tugging. One nipple was about to pop free from constraint. 'Hungry' didn't begin to describe it.

"But not here," she said, digging her knees hard into my midriff and straining away. I whoofed, groaned a complaint, and let her slide gradually down. One bent knee ground deliberately into my crotch as it went past, forcing out a different tone of groan.

"Think of the show we're putting on for anybody watching our shadows through the canvas," she said, once her feet were on the ground.

"We could just turn the damned light off," I said. "Or, what the hell, sell tickets to the show."

Carla scooped up a handful of the metal clamps that had held balloons to the wires strung along the backboard. "Nope." But she did turn out the light. "For what I have in mind, we'd knock the whole booth over, if you're as strong as you think you are."

That got my attention all right. So did the clamps. "So where are we going?" All I had to offer was a few not-so-clean blankets in a horse trailer, or a bunk in an RV that might fill up with randy teenagers at any moment. *Smooth. Really smooth, Casanova.*

"To my cheap, tacky motel room. Where else?" She edged through the canvas flap into the night still bright with streaks of garish colored light from the rides, and throbbing with the heavy beat of music. I followed, choosing strong-and-silent over the distinct possibility of making a fool of myself.

Her car was battered and dented. Prying open the passenger side door might have been a test of strength in itself, but, if so, I passed. Carla's skirt was hitched up so high in the driver's seat that I didn't refuse the invitation to explore beyond her garters, in the process making sure I'd know how to either unhook them with one hand when the time seemed right, or to work right past them. I couldn't recall anyone at vet school ever wearing garters. So much for getting into her panties; she wasn't wearing any.

From the pungent wetness of my fingers when we reached the motel, I knew Carla'd been more distracted than any driver should be, but when I tried to clinch just inside the door she pushed me away. "My room, my rules," she said sternly.

"We'll see," I said, leaning back against the closed door. Skin flushed, lips full and moist, heat practically radiating from her thighs, Carla clearly wanted it as much as I did. "What've you got in mind? Something like 'The bigger they come, the harder they fall'?"

"And the harder they come," she said, her purr verging on a growl. "Get on the bed."

Well, what else was I here for? I strode over, trying to look like it was my own idea. Then I saw what was fastened to the metal posts of the bed. "Wait a minute, aren't those the strings of beads I won?"

She reached into her purse. "Plenty more where those came from." Her voice became a falsetto caricature of a Mardi Gras reveler. "Hey, baby, show me your tits and I'll throw you some beads!"

I laughed, and shrugged out of my jacket, making sure the small tin of horse lube from my vet kit didn't fall out of its pocket. Then I plopped down on the bed. "Show you my tits? If you can't find 'em on your own, baby, maybe you better go back and practice on your balloons."

She launched herself forward. I was flat on my back, jeans unzipped and yanked down past my ass, shirt pulled way up and nipples firmly twisted between her fingers, before I could do more than grunt.

"Spread 'em," she ordered, kneeing me without mercy. "Arms too." She let go of my tits to push my hands toward the corners of the bed, which of course let her tempting breasts hang right above my mouth.

I went along with it. "You're going to tie me with just those flimsy strings of beads?"

"That's the plan." She got right to it. "Sure, you're thinking you can break free any time. But if you do, you lose out. The challenge is to hold still, no matter what I do to you." She reversed direction to work on tying my ankles. Now her crotch, skirt pushed up to her hips, was right above my face. I breathed in her scent hungrily, but didn't try to arch up toward her. I definitely didn't want to lose out.

So I lay still, if not silent, when the clamps came out. She moved them along my flesh like crab claws traveling across a dune, digging into my belly, my ribs, the lower swell of my breasts. Anticipation became as sharp as sensation, until my nipples seemed to be straining toward the promise of pain. When the metal bit into my tender peaks with cold fire, my stifled scream had as much of relief in it as anguish.

My shoulders clenched, my chest heaved, but I managed to keep my arms and legs nearly still. Carla watched my face, and bent to chew my lips when they twisted with the effort to be silent.

"Not bad," she muttered against my mouth, "for starters." Her tongue nudged at my gritted teeth until I relaxed them and let her probe deeply. The sheet under my hips grew hot and damp as I imagined that supple tongue probing elsewhere.

Carla finally reared back and released the clamps. Pain flooded back into areas that had become nearly numb. Then I felt the procession of crab pinches travel up my inner thighs. "How're we doing?" she asked cheerfully, bending her head to watch her handiwork.

"Next time," I gasped, "How about a room with a mirror on the ceiling?" Her head was dipping lower. Was that brief pinch on my pussy lips from metal, or fingers? And was that... oh God! Hot, wet, thrusting deep, and deeper, her face hidden between my thighs... My hips arched, my cunt grasped at the pressure, but Carla's tongue retreated, flicking my clit enough to swell it to desperation, but not quite to ignition.

"Don't move!" she said, and kept at me, teasing with darting tongue and pinching fingers until my throat was raw with groans and curses. But I must not have moved hard enough to break the strings of beads, because they still hadn't snapped.

Until suddenly she pressed harder, and deeper, hands under my ass pressing me upward toward the mouth that gave me everything I wanted, everything I could take. My wrists and ankles tore free as I forgot everything but the fierce, consuming bite of orgasm.

"Is that what you call losing out?" I said faintly, when I got enough breath back.

"You did okay," Carla said. "Look at your wrists."

They were scraped and bleeding, and so were my ankles. The damned strands of beads hadn't been so easy to break after all. "Looks like... looks like I didn't meet your challenge as well as I thought."

She shrugged. "Those suckers are tougher than you'd think. Nylon string, knots between each bead. There's a fastener on each necklace that just pops open, but once you release that and tie 'em like rope they're really strong. Don't go thinking something's flimsy just because it looks tacky and flashy and cheap."

"I don't see anything here tacky and flashy and cheap," I said. And meant it.

Carla leaned back and spread her thighs. The garters and belt had disappeared somewhere along the line.

"Show me what you got, then, big girl," she said, "and tomorrow I'll meet any challenge you name. Even if it means getting up close and personal with horses as big as elephants and twice as mean."

So I did, with hands that were hard where she was softest, leaving bruises to be savored for days. Finally, my fingers slicked with the horse lube, I worked my way deep into the first cunt I'd known that could swallow me to the wrist and clamp hard enough to give me bruises of my own. Not that I noticed those until much later, or the marks of her nails on my shoulders.

And Carla did meet her own challenge. Molly's broad black back will never look more glorious than it did when a dark-haired, seductive, naked Lady Godiva rode her through the horse barns one unforgettable midnight at the county fair.

THE FIRST PEONIES
IVY NEWMAN

The heavy bass of the music settles low in Holly's stomach, pulsing in rhythm as she surveys the club with a practiced eye. She takes a swig of her Jack and Coke, letting the glass hang loosely at her side as her gaze flickers over the dancers on the floor. It's a song for grinding, and the whole club seems to be undulating. The air is charged and fevered, and a light tack of sweat sheens Holly's skin, making the leather of her jacket stick slightly, despite her only wearing a thin gray t-shirt underneath it. She puts one hand in the pocket of the jacket, her moist fingers running over the fabric. It's comforting, the weathered leather supple from Holly's mother's repeated wear. Holly sighs, knocking back another gulp of her drink.

"Want a refill, Holly?" Matthew inquires from his position behind the bar. "Or do you want to stay sharp tonight?" Holly snorts softly, and brushes a stray tendril of black hair from her face. It's sweltering. Her jeans are clinging just shy of uncomfortably, but she leans casually on an elbow on Matthew's counter. He wipes down around her.

"Shut up," she says, although it's without heat. Matthew has become a friend over the few months Holly's been in the area. He helped her out when the drinks were flowing a little too freely one night. She woke up on his couch, clothed and comfortable, the morning after. He made eggs, and only laughed sparingly at her bed head. "It's a club. Everyone is here for the same thing; I'm not exactly a special case."

"Not everyone," Matthew says, smirking and indicating behind Holly with a flick of his eyebrows. She swivels and scans the vast mass of writhing bodies. The song has changed to something more upbeat, and anyone who didn't get too caught up in the last song's grinding is now jumping around and actually dancing. For a second, Holly doesn't see what Matthew's talking about, but then off to the right, she catches it.

A girl, short and curvy to Holly's tall and athletic, flails mindlessly among a circle of her friends. Although, 'friends' might be an overstatement, considering they're letting her make a fool of herself. Her arms swing so freely it's surprising they don't fly off and concuss anyone in her radius. Her hips are swiveling in a manner that Holly can only think of as the exact opposite of seductive, and her feet are doing something complicated and too varied to put any kind of name or reason to.

A laugh swells and dies on Holly's lips as the girl's whirling brings her face into view, and Holly's breath catches in her throat. The girl's face is cast in the changing colors of the club's lights. A soft smile curves the edges of her lips, which bow so perfectly Holly can hear Cupid sighing in the distance. Her hair is auburn, like autumn leaves distilled, and falls in a choppy layered bob around her face. Her eyes are closed, and Holly stares at her, soaking in her expression.

Rapture.

"Oh," Matthew says behind her, leaning over the bar so he can say it in her ear. The air tickles Holly's face and she flinches away. "Now this is unexpected."

"What?"

"I didn't know that devoid of rhythm and entirely awkward was your type, that's all." Holly rolls her eyes. She doesn't have a type. She has sex. Lots of it. Sex is fun, and a good stress relief. Making someone feel amazing, and them doing the same for you. It's basic. Easy.

"Shove it." Holly says, turning her focus back to the dance floor, only to find her pinwheel of a girl missing. She squashes the disappointment. There are loads of other girls here; she won't be going home alone. Unless she gets fixated on some whirling daydream of a thing. With a sigh, Holly pushes off the bar, and pulls a pack of cigarettes out of the back pocket of her jeans.

"Where are you off to, lady killer? You haven't picked up anyone yet."

Holly doesn't look back, flipping Matthew off over her shoulder with the hand holding the cigarettes and trusting he gets the message. She smiles. Matthew gets it; he's the perfect undemanding friend, taking Holly's caustic wit at face value. He never asks personal questions, not even the night he peeled her out of the club's bathrooms with eyeliner tracing a path down her cheeks.

Holly takes a deep breath when she gets outside into the alley next to the club, though regrets it immediately when the smell of garbage tickles at her nostrils. She lights her cigarette and inhales, watching the tendrils of smoke that escape her mouth tease and curl around the stars pinpricking the velvety night sky. They twinkle, clouded only for a second before the smoke is swept down to join the other scents in the alley.

Holly picks out the constellations idly, reciting them softly like mantras under her breath. The stars didn't taste like nicotine when she reclined on a picnic blanket as a child with her mother, only of hot chocolate and marshmallows. She remembers following the line of her mother's extended arm as she traced imaginary lines between each sparkling dot. The memory grows as foul in her mouth as the cigarette, as she recalls the growing lines of scars up that same arm. Her mother had carved herself away, had never quite managed to see the hope in all the stars she pointed to.

With no one left to teach her, neither did Holly.

Holly is yanked from her reverie by someone pushing open the side door, the club leaking the pumping bass into the alley. Holly glances up and finds herself looking at her pinwheel girl. The girl practically trips over her own feet getting out of the club, even though she's wearing wedged boots rather than heels. Her skirt cinches at her waist, emphasizing the curve of her hips, the hem swaying just above mid-thigh. Her tights are sheer black, and her shirt is denim, buttoned up to the collar. She glances Holly's way and her eyes widen slightly.

Her eyes. Holly's never seen anything quite like them; they're a perfect cornflower blue in the bright exit light. Also, staring equally intently at Holly.

Holly clears her throat, but refuses to break the intense eye contact they have. It's charged and electric, and is only made more so when the girl blushes, peachy and beautiful. She looks away, just for a moment, and then it's gone. "Do you have any spare?" she asks, gesturing to Holly's cigarette. Her voice is surprising. Holly was expecting something sweet, as if birds helped her get dressed that morning, but instead received the cadence of a jazz singer, mellow and with a slightly raspy edge. She feels her face heat up, and is grateful she isn't as disposed to a blushing complexion as this girl is.

Holly pulls out another cigarette, and passes it to the girl, letting her fingers brush against hers. Holly watches as the girl pulls it in between her lips. "Light?" They're standing so close together, Holly can see the elevated pace of the rise and fall of the girl's chest, and the way her blush is becoming a permanent stain, like watercolor on porcelain. Her eyelashes fan across her cheek as she blinks shyly, and Holly lets a smirk form on her own mouth. This at least is familiar territory.

Holly takes the girl's face gently in her hand, and turns it to tilt up to her own. Holly leans forward, and lets the tip of the lit cigarette in her mouth touch against the one between the girl's lips, waiting for the embers to light it. It catches, though Holly only knows by the flare of the glow, glaring in the relative dark of the alley. She's somewhat preoccupied with returning the girl's hooded gaze.

"Thanks," the girl says, as they pull away from each other. It comes out shaky, and Holly doesn't feel like she's faring much better. She feels like a novice, her knees practically knocking together, heat building in her underwear without even having done anything.

"No problem," she returns. They smoke, side by side, leaning against the wall of the club, not speaking. Holly's cigarette dwindles down to the butt, and she flicks it away, opening her mouth to say something further, to find the girl is already looking at her. Heatedly.

"My friends said you were watching me dancing," she says. *Better friends than I thought.*

"Maybe I was." The girl looks at Holly skeptically, Holly acquiesces. "I was." The girl's eyes turn calculating, as if she's scanning Holly for something. Bad intentions? Lies? Holly feels laid bare by her scrutiny, exposed and raw like an open nerve. She refuses to fidget. The girl seems satisfied by whatever she finds, though, leaning closer into Holly's space.

"Do you want to go somewhere with me?" the girl says, with a casual lilt to her voice that doesn't really come off.

"Yeah. Yeah, I do." Holly pauses. She registers a slight shock when she realizes what she wants. "What's your name?" Holly never asks for names if they're not offered. Holly never asks for anything, period. Take what you're given, get out before the dust settles, that's how she does things. Keep it basic and simple, always leave first.

"Mira," the girl says, and Holly's internal monologue dissipates into nothing.

"Holly," she returns, and doesn't dwell on the inexplicable fondness she's feeling, and how obviously it shows in her voice. It's impossible to dwell on anything at all when Mira smiles bright and unabashed, tossing her cigarette to the ground. She takes Holly's hand and tugs her out on to the main street, telling Holly about her car and how she hasn't been drinking. "My place is pretty close to here," she says, and her blush resurfaces. Holly doesn't pull her hand back. She doesn't want to. Her heart skips.

The thoughts tumble one after the other, and before she knows it, Holly is strapped into Mira's car, and they're driving in silence. The streetlights cast interrupted yellow light on them both in urban Morse code. Holly feels wrong in her skin, jumpy and erratic, and can't quite figure out why. She takes a breath, steeling herself, determined to take control of the situation again. Holly is not new to this, hasn't been new to this in a long time. Calming her expression, she relaxes her mouth and eyebrows. She is aloof and in control.

Holly reaches across the car's console, inching slowly. Mira doesn't notice until Holly's hand snakes onto her thigh, and then Mira's breath hitches audibly at the contact. Holly rubs her hand back and forth, slowly, controlling her own breathing and reactions carefully. She lets her hand slide down to the hem of Mira's skirt, and draws it back. Mira's hands tighten on the steering wheel, and Holly allows herself a small smile. *This is more like it.* She curves her hand further in, pulling Mira's legs apart before tracing small circles on Mira's inner thigh, delighting in the growing heaviness in her breath. It's deafening in the silence of the car, neither of them having

88

said a word since they got in.

Holly expands the circles to figure eights, changing which finger she uses as if she's changing keys on a piano. It's effortless, and the barrier of the tights between their skins is tantalizing. Holly traces closer and closer to Mira's underwear. She runs her index finger lightly along the seam, and Mira takes a sharp breath. "This okay?" Holly murmurs, getting tingly and warm herself. Mira nods jerkily, and Holly moves her finger more purposefully, though still with a teasing pace and pressure. She continues caressing, following Mira's breathing and the occasional sigh like a roadmap.

They pull into an apartment complex, and Mira finally turns to look at Holly. Her pupils are dilated, only the outermost edge of blue to be seen. Her face is flushed and gorgeous. The effect is ruined by the look of abject terror.

"Hey," Holly says, withdrawing her hand quickly, "We don't have to do anything if you don't w-"

"No! I want to. I really want to." Holly is momentarily gratified by the flick of Mira's eyes up and down her body. "I just, I've never done *this*."

"This?"

"Brought a stranger home. It's the first time." She looks down at her lap, apparently fascinated by her hands as they lay clasped there. "I'm more of a relationship person, but when my friends pointed you out to me, I guess I thought..."

Holly smiles, pulling Mira's face to hers, just as she did when she was lighting her cigarette. She moves in close, and lets her lips rest on Mira's without kissing. Just resting, her mouth against that perfect bow.

"There's a first time for everything," Holly finishes Mira's thought in a whisper, their lips brushing like a promise. There's a second of hesitation before Mira swells up to meet her, threading her hands through

Holly's dark tresses. Holly sucks Mira's lower lip into her mouth, and receives a nibble in return. It's a perfect to and fro, and by the time their tongues are touching, Holly's forgotten everything about the concept of breathing, not wanting to pause, even for a second. It's sweet and fast, and Holly feels everything inside her roiling and tumbling, her ribcage housing an approaching storm. She's lost in Mira's mouth, and is even more lost when she finally pulls away. Mira inhales slowly, and retracts her hands from Holly's hair.

"Let's go," she says with finality, and is out of the car with a swish of her skirt and the lingering smell of what Holly thinks might be peonies. She allows herself a second. *Peonies.* Holly is rough edges, too much whiskey, cigarette stained fingernails and just broken enough that it's not endearing. This girl is peonies and autumnal rain showers and she wants *Holly*.

Holly jumps out of the car and follows Mira.

Door.

Elevator.

Mira. As soon as she closes the apartment door behind them, Holly takes her by the waist and spins her around. She pushes Mira back against the door, and leans, fully flush against her body. She drowns herself in Mira's mouth again, knows there's a dealer's market to be had in her lips. They part, and Holly plants a row of open-mouthed kisses along Mira's jaw, working her way to her throat. She sucks a mark where she can feel Mira's pulse jumping, and feels connected to her. Holly has always craved the buzz of sex, the tingling and warmth of it. Mira makes her feel like a live wire.

She runs her hands up and down Mira's sides, and unbuttons the top button at the collar of her shirt, letting her finger trace the dip of the hollow of her throat. She lifts up from Mira's neck. "Bedroom?" Mira nods frantically, and starts pushing Holly back by the shoulders. Her hands drift beneath the fabric of Holly's jacket, pushing it off and leaving it lying on the floor. Holly feels a slight twinge at leaving it there, but doesn't go back for it. Mira takes her hand and drags her into the bedroom.

The curtains are open, the room lit by a dim lamp on the bedside locker and the streams of moonlight and stars. Holly kicks off her boots as they stumble toward the bed, and falls on top of Mira, their legs twining together. She deftly unbuttons the rest of Mira's shirt, sliding it off her shoulders. She straddles Mira, and pulls her shirt over her head. Mira lays a hand flat against Holly's stomach, reaching up between her breasts and back down again, as if she's drinking Holly in through her fingers. Her hair is mussed as if they've been rolling around for hours rather than minutes, and Holly wants to see what it looks like after a bit more time. Holly yearns for dishevelment.

She slides down the length of Mira's body, trailing kisses along her torso as she goes, then kneels at her feet. Holly picks up Mira's foot, and divests her of her boots, throwing them carelessly over her shoulder. The *thunk* of them hitting the carpet startles her into speaking. "You are gorgeous," she says, voice low and devastatingly reverent. She reaches up and hooks her fingers into the waistband of Mira's tights and underwear, dragging them down over her legs, watching the trail of goose bumps that follow. Holly scratches lightly down the length of Mira's legs. She watches her squirm. "Just perfect."

"Why are you still wearing so many clothes?" Mira asks. Holly laughs and Mira's pout evolves into something affectionate. It hurts as if Holly's looking directly into the sun, but she can't bring herself to look away.

"Take off your skirt and I'll see what I can do about this situation." Holly gestures down at herself, and pops the button of her jeans. Mira's eyes become hooded again and they both clamber to get out of their remaining clothes. They're falling together again in no time, two heartbeats in what feels like one ribcage.

Holly is taken aback when Mira rolls them so that she's on top, and smirks down at Holly. She slithers down until her face is level with Holly's breasts, the display of grace so unexpected from the girl who had been careening around the dance floor like a spinning top earlier in the night. Holly likes both versions of her, she decides, especially when Mira circles one of Holly's nipples with her tongue. Holly hears a moan escape from her own mouth when Mira starts to suck, gently squeezing Holly's other nipple between delicate fingers. Heat pools between her legs, and another noise wrests itself from her throat. Mira lifts her head, and Holly narrowly avoids whining at the loss.

"You make the best sounds," Mira says, her raspy voice growing hoarser by the minute. She slips her hand down Holly's stomach again and stops at her cunt, teasing the lips open. Holly feels simultaneously afloat, and irrevocably weighted in her body. It's almost painful how much she wants this.

She moans aloud when Mira starts to rub Holly's clit, changing the pace and pattern often and without warning. Holly's head is spinning, and she can hear herself getting louder under Mira's seemingly endless ministrations. Mira leans down to steal a kiss, and Holly twines her arms around Mira's neck, fingers tangling in her short hair. Mira swallows every sound and her fingers speed up deliciously. Holly has never had a partner this attentive; she follows every twitch of Holly's legs, responds to every noise. Holly has felt wanted, sure, desired in the past, but never so wholly taken care of. Her hips buck up into every stroke and touch, chasing the sensation. Her legs tense to the point of spasm as she comes, her last moan torn from her throat, melting into the quiet of the room. She opens her eyes slowly, coming down to find Mira looking down at her reverence in her gaze. "Beautiful," she says, her voice absolutely wrecked, even though Holly was the one making all the noise. Holly takes Mira's hand, the one that turned Holly to jelly just moments before, and sucks the taste of herself from Mira's expert fingers. Mira's eyes are impossibly dark, and her pupils are blown wide with anticipation, the room filled with the heady scent of sex.

Now it is Mira's turn. Holly had been planning on something quick and dirty, something to appeal to whatever sense of adventure Mira might be trying to appease with her first one-night stand. But now, Holly knows that isn't what she wants. So, Holly leans up, and kisses the tip of Mira's nose, and while she is still surprised, rolls her onto her back, fluffing up the pillows around her head. She makes her comfortable, and takes in the sight of her body, softness and curves. Holly has always been about dirty rooms and dirtier people, knowing she belongs there. Feeling like she doesn't belong anywhere else. But not this time, she thinks; this time, peonies.

Holly takes one last slow kiss from Mira's perfect lips, and slides down the length of her body. She parts Mira's legs, and nestles between them, feeling like this may be where she belongs after all. Mira looks down at her, and the way she does it makes Holly feel like some kind of goddess. She dives in, parting Mira's folds and dipping her tongue in experimentally, to see what Mira likes. If the sudden yet slight arch to her back is any indication, she likes the flicking around her clit, and the sucking, the light, teasing nibbles to her folds. She isn't loud the way Holly is loud. It seems, as Holly noticed in the car, it's all about breath for Mira. Holly chases the exquisite, sharp intakes, the long breathy sighs, the too loud exhalations. She plays Mira like a finely tuned harp, working toward that crescendo. When it comes, Mira's spine bows, and her hands fist in Holly's hair, urging her on. Holly moans deep into Mira, and maybe it's the reverberation that does it, but Mira's thighs are trembling around Holly's ears and her breath stops entirely.

Slowly, Mira withdraws her hand from Holly's hair and sags into the nest of pillows Holly made for her. Holly wipes her mouth and grins, climbing back up the bed to curl into Mira's side. Mira seems too out of it to really respond, but takes Holly's hand in hers, shaking a little as she does. Her chest still rises and falls rapidly, and they don't speak until she catches it. Mira turns to face Holly, and Holly drinks in the sight of her face, flushed and perfect, her hair a mess, and all of her, every perfect square inch, drenched in starlight. Mira sighs. "That was amazing," she says, her voice ragged. "Thank you."

Holly's face drops, she can't help it. It sounds sincere, but Holly can't take any satisfaction from it, because it's also final. Holly rolls out of the bed and starts looking for her clothes. She shrugs. "No problem," she says, as if her heart isn't cracking, shattering as she hooks her bra and tries to keep her dignity, whatever can be said to still belong to her. She hopes the slight tremor in her voice sounds like the effects of the afterglow rather than what it is.

"Holly?" She turns around, careful to keep her expression neutral. Mira looks vulnerable, her legs curled up, and she's draped her shirt back over herself, crossing her arms protectively. She looks unerringly into Holly's eyes. "Look, I know this was a one-night stand, I get that, and I said that's what I wanted. I'm okay with it if you just want to leave." She pauses, and looks with the same critical eye she had outside the club, and Holly feels just as naked as she did then, maybe even more so. "But I kind of feel like maybe you don't want to leave."

Holly can't say anything to that. She feels paralyzed by indecision, by fear.

"Maybe you could stay the night? We could get breakfast in the morning and I don't know... talk? Get to know each other."

Holly's heart is beating a fast, steady rhythm. *Run, run, run.*

But looking at the curve of Mira's bare calves and the way her pupils are contracted in the moonlight, she realizes something that makes her heart flip over and her stomach drop. She pulls against the tide of fear and the rules about always leaving first. Leave before they leave you. Break hearts to remain unbroken. Holly's mother's jacket lies on the floor of Mira's living room and it's time. It's time Holly wades into the murky waters of trust, takes a swan dive into faith. This isn't the first time Holly's gone home with a stranger, not by a long shot. But it is the first time she's wanted to stay.

She nods jerkily, and drops her jeans back to the floor. She pulls her shirt over her head and climbs into the sheets of Mira's bed, cool and smooth against her bare legs. Mira climbs in after her and they curl into each other, Mira's face graced with a soft smile Holly wants to kiss, to whisper against, and be utterly consumed by.

I will stay, she thinks, *for as long as she'll let me.*

REPOSSESSION
EMILY L. BYRNE

I was looking around the house when it hit me: Lydia Chang from the bank said that she'd be here at 3:00 p.m. to pick up the keys and it was 2:30 p.m. now. I had to be ready but I wasn't even sure what that meant anymore. Ready to hand over the house and the keys? Or ready to deal with Lydia? Either way, I was screwed.

The furniture was already gone, sold off or put into storage. I'd cleaned a little, enough to spare what was left of my pride. Mom would be proud that I tried, once she started talking to me again. I wandered through what had been my home for two years and I thought about my ex. Then I thought about divorce and balloon payments and what a dirty word "foreclosure" really was.

Marcella could have at least come down to say goodbye to all this. And to me. I rubbed my hands over my head, pricking my fingertips on the razor stubble. How the hell did I end up here? And why had I shaved my head? My scalp wasn't telling and neither were the empty rooms. A deep wave of utter despair threatened to suck me under.

I remembered Marcella standing at the sink in the kitchen, chopping vegetables. I remembered coming home and slipping up behind her, holding her close while I buried my face in her hair. God, I loved the way she smelled: spices and soap, and the indefinable aftermath of sex. Even when it wasn't with me. Of course, I didn't know that at the time.

I slid down the wall and sat on the bare floor, curling my arms over my head. They'd said I didn't have to do it this way but I wanted to turn the house over personally; no mailed or dropped off keys for me. Anything for one last little bit of control. The truth was that I couldn't let it go that easily: not the house or Marcella or any of it, and I was even willing to risk the humiliation of dealing with Lydia Chang just to spend more time with my old life.

I tried to brace myself for what was coming, mere moments away. Conveniently enough, at least for her schedule, Lydia Chang didn't even live that far away. Her house was only a mile or so away from our little south-side Dyke Heights neighborhood. All one big happy family and none of them free to help me out today.

Of course, I wasn't being fair. As usual. Ruby and Sharon were letting me crash on their couch until I could find something else, and they weren't the only ones being nice. But right now, I felt like the loneliest dyke in the world. But then, this was also what I got for saying I could handle things without help. I had literally no idea what I was thinking. Whatever it had been, I wasn't thinking it now.

I tilted my head back to look at the textured ceiling I'd never gotten around to smoothing over. I followed a crack over and down the wall and wondered if the next owners would patch that up. When new owners finally bought the place, that is. I sure hadn't had any luck selling it when I put it on the market.

I'd tried to keep making payments after I threw Marcella out, but then I got laid off and got too far in the hole for any help from the city. Hell of a year all around, full of all the worst kinds of firsts that a gal could have. I thumped my head against the wall and tried to focus on the good.

Now at least I had a new job, too late to do

anything about the house but at least I could get an apartment as soon as I found one. That was something. Ruby and Sharon weren't going to want me on their couch forever, although they kept saying otherwise. But then that was what good friends did: took you in and put you up even after you yelled at them for suggesting that your girlfriend was a lying, cheating bitch with money management problems.

I missed her anyway. Because hot sex and house and love and everything. I banged my head harder against the wall. But only once. There was no point in knocking my brains any looser than they were already.

For no particular reason, that got me thinking about why Ms. Lydia Chang, bank officer, had agreed to come over here at all. The story was that she owed Sharon a favor but Sharon wouldn't tell me just what that favor was. It had to be big. Ms. Chang and I had some history, at least if you called a couple of disaster dates back when I first moved to town 'history'.

I moved on. She didn't, not for a while, and it made things awkward, what with the glaring and the sniping on her part and the guilty indifference on mine. Our paths hadn't crossed again for a couple of years, and I'd heard she'd gotten into banking in the meantime. But just my luck, she stayed friends with Sharon and Sharon called in a favor. Or something.

I wondered what Ms. Chang thought about at times like these. Did it piss her off to foreclose on people and watch their dreams go down the tubes? Or was she just numb to it all? And as long as I was at it, I wondered if she'd like to take me out to dinner sometime, for old time's sake. She'd probably be thrilled I was the one that got away.

Truthfully, I still thought Lydia was pretty hot, in a severe social top sort of way. It was just that our personalities were like ice and fire. And as far as I knew, she still hated me. So maybe she was doing this for the sheer fun of watching me bleed. The last thought snapped me out of my funk in time to hear the doorbell.

I got up slowly, trying and failing to say goodbye to everything in my head. I even dumped the beer down the drain so I wouldn't look as buzzed and belligerent as I actually felt. Then I shuffled off to open the door. Ms. Chang's unsmiling face appeared, framed by the downtown skyline in the background. "Hi," I said, in a cheery voice that didn't even convince me.

She stepped up from the porch into the foyer, her body trim and sleek in a navy blue suit that reminded me of armor. Once she got inside, she studied me, looking from my shaved head down to my grubby tennis shoes. I felt like an interesting new specimen that she'd just discovered.

I wished I'd taken a shower after I finished cleaning. I was afraid that she could see what I had been thinking and I tried to wipe my face clean of thoughts lustful or otherwise. Then the moment passed and she gave me her smooth banker's smile and one slender hand to shake. Just as if we'd never met before. "Good afternoon, Ms. Carroll."

I shook her hand carefully and let go quickly. This was all kinds of creepy, but at least it didn't require any emotional involvement on my part. I should get this over with fast, and play along; that much was clear.

She gestured upstairs. "Shall we?"

I froze, something that was not quite butterflies dancing in my stomach. Did I have to give her a tour or something? It wasn't supposed to work like this. Give her the keys and the signed papers, they said; they'd get back to me about any problems. So what was this? "I have to show you the house?"

"Certainly you don't have to, but I'd like you to." Ms. Chang smiled and gave me another sidelong head to toe glance that sent a curious wave of sensation from my belly down to my thighs. It was probably just wishful thinking but suddenly I very much wanted to show her the house, or at least the upstairs. I started climbing the stairs.

"Stop." Her voice froze me in place.

"What?" I was getting baffled.

"Why don't you tell me about this staircase?"

Now I was really baffled. I mean, stairs were stairs. "Not sure what you want to know, but it goes from this hallway to the second floor hallway. The carpet's original, unfortunately, so it's pretty worn in spots. The third tread creaks..." Her face wasn't giving me any kind of hint so I kept prattling until I ran out of steam.

"Tell me about this staircase and Marcella."

Oh shit, that traveled fast! I whipped around and got nose to nose with Lydia. "I don't know who the hell you think you are but that is none of your damn business!"

She crossed her arms and frowned. Her look took me in from stubble to grubby sneakers and made me feel wanting, in all kinds of ways. Her foot tapped the stair tread as she waited. "Tell me," she said in a voice that was no longer a request.

"Fuck you." She didn't blink. We glared at each other until something inside me crumbled. After all, what was a little more humiliation? It wasn't like it would get much worse. I sat on the step and put my face in my hands. "I came home to find her here, on the stairs with her lover." Then I added, under my breath, "Now I'm losing my house to you because I have the worst taste in women on the planet."

She must not have heard that last part. "What were they doing?" Lydia, no, Ms. Chang, held up one hand. "No, don't tell me. Show me."

I yanked my hands into my lap and gaped at her.

For the first time, I noticed that her white blouse was unbuttoned a bit farther than bank officer standard. Her skirt was shorter and the look in her eyes wasn't saying 'banker' to me. What the hell was going on here? My heart started to race. Was this some sort of new kink I'd never heard of? Or something else?

We stared at each other for some very long minutes until I decided that whatever we were doing couldn't possibly make me feel any worse. "Well, Marcella was lying back on the stairs like this." I stretched back and spread my legs. Then I flashed back to the look on my ex's face while her new girlfriend ate her pussy. I could feel the tears start.

"Unbutton your jeans."

I shut my eyes to hold them in but they trickled down my cheeks anyway. I fumbled with my buttons while she watched, lost in my bad memories. Then I dragged my hands over my face and waited with my eyes closed for whatever came next. What did I have to lose at this point?

"I want you to put two of your fingers inside yourself and rub your clit with your thumb. Then finish telling me what happened."

My eyes popped open and I stared at her. She raised one eyebrow and smiled, just a bit, and that look sent chills down my spine. My first humiliation scene; how lucky could a gal get in a single day? I wondered if she did this with all her clients. Then I wondered what else my so-called friends had told her.

I put my hand down my pants and did what she told me. My hips bucked the minute I touched myself and the electric shock rippled from my clit down my legs. I gasped. How had she known? An impatient sound made me remember that my audience was waiting. I couldn't forget that. "Marcella was lying here with her pants down around her ankles. Jody's face was between her thighs and I could hear her sucking on Marcella's clit."

"Did Marcella get to come on the stairs?"

"No. I walked in on them and started yelling."

"Then you don't get to come here either. Show me the upstairs. No, leave your jeans unbuttoned."

I yanked up my pants and stumbled up the stairs in a daze, wondering why she was doing this. And wondering what to show her next. I picked the bathroom because it was closest.

"And what did you do here?" Ms. Chang's voice purred, at once too close and too far away.

I closed my eyes and tried to remember happier times, before my life turned to shit. Way back, when we first bought the house, Marcella and I used this shower to... "Yes?" The banker's peeved tone inserted itself into my memories and shredded them. I blinked at her, with no idea why she was frowning at me until I looked down. My hand was already back inside my pants. I jerked it out.

"Umm... yeah. When we first moved in here, Marcella came in while I was showering and..." That was when the despair hit me again and I slumped against the wall of what used to be my house and thought about everything I had lost.

Ms. Chang was pitiless. "And what happened?"

I thought about screaming at her and storming out. It would have been appropriate. Why the hell was I entertaining the woman who was taking away the one thing I had left? I glared at her fiercely and she met my glare head on, no readable expression on her face. "Why are you doing this?"

"I want you to show me what you will remember of your life here. I want you to be able to let it all go when you leave."

"Sharon put you up to this, didn't she?" I was breathing hard now. "Well, you can just stop."

"I don't want to stop. I want to finish going through the house with you. What happened in this room that you want to leave here, Ms. Carroll?" Her voice was cool, detached but I could see her breath catch a little. Her tongue darted out and licked her lips, a gesture that combined longing and uncertainty somehow. It put me over the edge.

"You want to know what happened in here? Fine! I walked in on Marcella in the shower and took her, right over there against that wall. She screamed my name louder than she'll ever scream Jody's and we went back to the bedroom and fucked all day. That hot enough for you?" I was yelling now, the ache between my legs forgotten.

Lydia looked me straight in the eye, lips parted to catch her breath. I could see her cleavage now when I glanced down her blouse. "Show me." She said it very softly, so quietly I almost didn't hear her.

I reached out and grabbed her, kissing her so hard our mouths nearly fused together. My hands tore at her suit, dragging the jacket off her, then popping the buttons off her blouse as I yanked it off. She moaned as I picked her up and stepped into the tub with her. She kicked her heels off as I set her down and turned on the water, soaking us both. Then I pulled her skirt up over her hips and yanked down her panties.

She was leaning back against the wall now, her fingers digging into my skull, her eyes half closed. I stood, driving my hand into her hard enough that she yelped. Then I raised her hands over her head and held them there while I kissed her again, wrapping her tongue in mine to swallow her moans. She was riding my hand now, her hips rocking back and forth with each of my thrusts.

My clothes were soaked through and I could feel her body through my wet t-shirt, feel her groan in my throat. I twisted my hand so that my thumb found her clit and I pressed down and rubbed until she surrendered to me, thighs shaking and head back in a soft growl. I kissed her neck, licking the soft skin as I kept thrusting until she came again, harder this time.

I pulled back and released her before I stepped, dripping, from the tub. "Was it hotter than that?" she murmured, still catching her breath.

"Much." I lied with every fiber of my being but I was too proud to tell her that.

"Then we're not done yet. Show me the next room." She picked up her wet shirt and pulled it back on, leaving it open over her lacy bra. Then she stepped out of the tub and back into the heels she had kicked off. I could hear her feet squish into them.

"You have got to be kidding me." The ache was back now and I wanted her badly, maybe even more than I had ever wanted Marcella. But I shouldn't and I knew it.

"Show me," she said, the command back in her voice even though her makeup streaked her cheeks and she was leaving a puddle on the floor with every step.

"Fine." I turned on my heel with a frustrated snarl and stomped over to the old office/guest room. "Once, we came in here during a barbecue and Marcella pushed me onto the bed and ate me out while our guests walked up and down the hallway outside." I wasn't telling the whole truth but I wanted this woman so badly now it didn't matter.

"You're lying. Tell me what really happened."

How the hell did she know? I took a deep breath and closed my eyes. "I walked in to see what had happened to her and Jody because they'd been gone a while. They weren't actually touching but they weren't standing far enough apart either. Jody took off and Marcella grabbed me and pulled me down on the bed on top of her." I was cringing inside now. How had I not known?

"Then what?" If she knew what I was figuring out, it didn't show.

"She put her thigh between mine and I rode it while I rubbed her off. Then we went back downstairs with big shit-eating grins on our faces."

"Like this?" She was in front of me now, forcing her wet thigh between mine. I crouched a little to make up for the difference in our heights and rocked against her. The sensation sent a lightning bolt through me and I moaned softly. "Hand between my legs, cowboy," she murmured into my ear, grabbing my hand and putting it where she wanted it.

She was soaking wet and I grinned as I kissed her, all the while the seam in my jeans was sending little jolts through my pussy. "I can't come standing up," I whispered into her ear just before I took her lobe between my teeth and bit it.

Her breath hissed through her teeth. "Tough." And she bit me back, catching the skin over my collarbone between her lips until I yelped. She pressed herself against me until I could feel her nipples harden against mine. She leaned down and took one of my breasts in her mouth, bending herself at an impossible angle while the pressure from her thigh became unbearable. I was on fire, gasping, hands buried in her hair while her insistent mouth drew a line of fire from nipple to clit.

It hit me all at once and my knees buckled as my legs shook too hard to hold me up without her support. I screamed when I came, howling out everything I wanted, everything I had lost. We slid down onto the floor in a wet quivering pile, with her more or less on my lap. I kissed her more gently now and she wiped a tear from my cheek. "Why are you doing this really?" I asked when I could talk again.

"Why do you think I'm doing it?"

"I think you feel sorry for me."

"This seems like a series of pity fucks to you? You think I got nothing better to do with my time, Ms. Carroll?" She dug her fingers into my scalp hard and tilted my head up so I had to look her in the eye.

It hurt but I got something like a clue. She was doing this because she wanted to and I was damn lucky that it was me she wanted and she might keep wanting me if I got my shit together. It still didn't make sense but I'd go along with it. And keep asking. She must have seen that in my expression because she got up and dragged me with her.

Then we were off to the bedroom. That was the worst of it, really, for me anyway. Even her tongue on my clit and her fingers crammed up inside me weren't enough to stop the hurt. I cried the whole time she kissed and licked me, but I came despite it all.

I even managed to go down on her, letting her scent and taste fill my mouth and nose until she was the whole world. Somewhere in there, I stopped being miserable. I licked and licked until it felt like my tongue was going to fall off and stay inside her. I was wondering if that was such a bad thing just as her back arched and she bucked against me, wailing as she shook. At least I wasn't losing my touch with the ladies.

Or was I? She grinned at me and pulled me up to her for a kiss once the aftershocks subsided but I didn't get the sense that she'd be renting a U-Haul. "So why did you do this?" I knew we were done for now; and post-coital snuggling was off the map.

"I'm guessing that you're making up a little story in your head about that, aren't you? Stick with that; the whole fiction you're creating about the kindly lesbian daughter of immigrants rejecting her banker day job to bring comfort to her distraught butch client is better than anything I could come up with. Reality can be so

107

mundane."

I raised an eyebrow. "So, you're psychic too?"

"No. You just have a very readable face." She grinned up at me. "I can't want a scene with my newly single hot butch client, all other considerations aside?"

I kissed her as I ran my hands over everything I could reach. "My original notion wasn't that Hollywood, believe me. But I think I'm glad you did this. Or I will be when I have a chance to think about it."

"Good. Me, too. I'll even forgive the 'worst taste in women on the planet' comment. Now let's go."

"This instant?"

"I've got paperwork to get back to." And there went my fantasy about dinner tonight, just like that. A few minutes later we were more or less dressed and standing on the porch. She locked the doors and put up the notice on the porch window. I trailed after her down the stairs, feeling desolate again.

"Can I see you again?" I tried not to whine, believe me. But there it was.

"When a woman is with me," Ms. Chang said, "I expect to be the only thing she sees when she shuts her eyes. You weren't ready for me the last time, and you're not ready now, not yet. Call me when that changes." And she walked away, still dignified despite the wreckage of her suit, the keys to what used to be my house jingling in her hand.

I let her go and take a bit of myself with her. I'd be working to get it back.

THAT SUMMER
VANESSA DE SADE

It was a hot, dry, sultry summer. A summer like no other. *Aladdin Sane* was in the charts, Britain was now in the Common Market, Greece became a Republic, and General Pinochet staged a coup against the democratically elected government of Chile. And, released from the parental leash for the first time, I met Mary. Mary, Mary, quite contrary. Such a plain and commonplace name for the person who turned my humdrum life around and taught me how to feel.

However, I'm getting ahead of myself...

I did not come from an ordinary household. My parents were both Party members and vocal critics of the reigning Conservative Heath government as people were back then. It was before the ease of on-line forums and one-click petitions, and they shouted their indignation on the streets with other pipe-smoking men in duffle coats, and longhaired women in Afghans and Bri-Nylon polo neck sweaters. My father was a teacher, hard working if a bit disheveled in his flared blue denims and green corduroy jacket. He risked instant dismissal to trundle out socialist leaflets on the school Banda duplicator in the murky chalk-dust hours of the early evening. My mother, an operating theater nurse, worked grueling shifts and came home bloody in the gray dawn-light of the small hours. Sometimes, she yearned for a life where she could just sit back and watch *The Sound of Music* and gossip with her friends, but was furiously angry at the same time as she choked back her indignation on an almost daily basis at the male-dominated infrastructure of the health service.

Then there was me. Angela Lenin Scott. (Seriously.) Born 3 August 1954. Girl. Only child and brutally neglected by my parents for the sake of the greater good. Imaginative, creative and incredibly smart. Living a fantasy life with my Sindy doll where my parents were dead—usually from a fatal road accident but sometimes nuclear holocaust—and where we both dressed in clothes from Chelsea Girl and traveled the world in a converted double-decker bus. I was a Leo according to the Zodiac. "Original, imposing, inflexible, motivated, ambitious, loyal, physical, charitable, and majestic." Or so the teenage magazines that I was forbidden to buy would have told me if I'd ever sneaked a peak.

Poetry should have been my passion, novels my very lifeblood, but the road to the arts was a rocky one in my household and paved with insurmountable obstacles. My father was a chemistry teacher, and had already mapped out a career in law for me, righting society's wrongs, and being the advocate of the masses, the voice of the disenfranchised. Or something like that, I forget the precise rhetoric. I had already read the hefty three-volume biography of Karl Marx on the dining room bookshelf by the time I was eleven, *Das Kapital* before I was even twelve. I devoured my parent's book of the month choices from the Left Book Club until the subscription ran out, mainly dull as dishwater political treatises within their bright yellow dust jackets, occasionally lengthy tomes of fictional struggle by long-dead Russians like Dostoevsky or Gogol. I smuggled what I could from the poorly stocked shelves of the local library, mainly torrid romances, and indifferently paced thrillers from the 1930s, to be read clandestinely by torchlight under the bedclothes late at night.

At school, I was bright and opinionated, breezing exams but never too popular with my teachers, and treated warily by my peers, who were all busy experimenting with cigarettes and alcohol, and losing their virginity, while I canvassed household after indifferent household with our badly printed socialist treatises, and joined my parents on picket lines and demonstrations at the weekend. I braved the winter of discontent within the confines of my cold bedroom under the watchful eye of the Free Angela Davis poster that my father never fully approved of. Protest was one thing, but that woman just went too far...

And then there was Mary and that fateful summer that almost never happened. My mother had volunteered to do a three-month VOS stint at a hospital in some unheard of now-several-times-renamed African state, my father also agreeing to do his bit teaching at the local school during the long summer vacation. I was eighteen going on nineteen, so the plan was that I too should come to Africa for the summer, as I had completed my schooling and was not—I think because it hadn't occurred to anyone—being farmed out to gain valuable experience in a socialist-approved legal aid law office before taking up my hard-earned place at St Andrew's University. And thus we were all duly vaccinated up the wazoo and back when the familiar theme tune of *News at Ten* echoed through the house and Sandy Gall's unsmiling features announced a military coup in our chosen destination, throwing all our carefully conceived plans out of the window.

My mother was adamant that she should still go. There would be casualties, she screamed. Hundreds of them. She would simply switch from the VOS program to the medical corps of the UN peacekeeping force. And my father had been a biochemist and trained as a health worker before his teaching days. There would be plenty for him to do there too...

That only left me, the single fly in their otherwise perfect socially conscious ointment. I was about to be shipped off to an elderly aunt for the duration, when a colleague of my mother's saved the day. Saved my life, actually.

Hugo MacDonald he was called. A consultant at the hospital where my mother worked. Suave, upper class, and erudite, his recent divorce had inspired him to take up good works to fill the long empty hours and now sent him to the dark continent to help patch-up its latest combat victims. However, he also owned a second home in the Scottish Highlands and he had planned to visit with his own daughter during what passed for the hot season in northern Britain.

"Listen, let the girls spend the summer together," he told my parents. My mother, enraptured by his muscular yachtsman's physique, tanned surgeon's hands, and deep gravelly voice; my father openly hostile but trying not to show it. "It's a secure cottage by a loch in the middle of nowhere and it's completely isolated so they can't possibly come to any harm. And Mary's already at St Andrew's so it'll be quite wonderful for your Angela, plus she'll have a friend to show her the ropes when she goes up to the university in the autumn."

"And what exactly is your daughter studying?" my father had asked, his irrational aggression toward this urbane man barely held in check.

"Political science," said the surgeon, and the deal was done.

* * *

The house, such as it was, was situated a mile or so down a dirt lane and clung perilously to the foreshore of its own tiny bay, invisible both from the road and the open expanse of azure blue water of the vast sea loch. There was a village of sorts, about three miles away, where there was a bright red telephone box for emergencies and a shop that sold milk and eggs and other basics. But standing against the stark blue of the huge cloudless canopy of sky, gulls wheeling above our heads with shrill cries, it was as if we were the last surviving humans on the planet.

Hugo kissed his daughter, shook my hand, and climbed, smiling, into his sleek blue Jaguar and drove smartly away, taking the last vestiges of civilization with him. We listened to the powerful engine labor its way slowly up the steep dirt track and eventually fade away to nothing. And I suddenly felt bereft.

"Come on, come inside and stow your stuff," Mary said to me with a friendly smile, as if reading my mind. "Then we need to gather some driftwood for the fire before we lose the sun. It gets chilly here after dark."

It wasn't at all what I'd been expecting. Just a basic brick and asbestos prefabricated bungalow dating back to World War II, plain-fronted, with a couple of rooms, and an outhouse toilet. There was a wood burning stove in the lounge, two gas mantle lights with a big red Calor gas cylinder out the back, a cupboard full of tinned food, and a single-ring stove to cook it on in the kitchen. The bedroom boasted two ex-army bunks, and an old wine bottle with a candle in it for light. But what caused me to fall in love with the place regardless was that every available surface was stacked high with tottering towers of paperback books.

* * *

The days passed slowly, luxuriantly, beautifully. We ate tinned soups and stews supplemented with wild raspberries and brambles that we picked from steep hillside thickets, the whole hillside ablaze with pink and purple rhododendrons. We hiked to the village and bought bread and butter and bars of chocolate, and, occasionally, a bottle of cheap red wine. We kept the woodpile stocked, and swam in the afternoons when the chill wind dropped and the hot sun had warmed the rocks and heated the water. Then we lay on the beach and talked. And talked, and talked, and talked.

Mary was my first real friend, first mentor, and the most wonderful person that I had ever met. She had cascades of long black hair that tumbled over her shoulders in a mass of gypsy curls, she wore little gold penny-round spectacles when she read, and smoked long slim Russian cigarettes in a rainbow hue of colors. She had read everything worth reading, and so she picked out book after book for me. George Orwell—banned in my house as a "traitor to the Left"—with his hard-hitting journalism and dystopian fiction. *The Collector* by John Fowles. *Lord of the Flies*. Poetry by Sylvia Plath, Anne Sexton, Elizabeth Smart. *The Bell Jar*. *Novel on Yellow Paper*. *By Grand Central Station I Sat Down and Wept*. Ernest Hemingway. F. Scott Fitzgerald. And then *Lolita*, *To Kill A Mockingbird* and *The Catcher in the Rye*.

"It's as if they've opened the top of my head and seen what's inside," I said to her, wiping the tears from my eyes at the conclusion of Holden Caulfield's sojourn to the dark side of 1950s New York. "It's like seeing my own thoughts spread out upon the page, or projected on a screen, like in that poem by Elliot."

Mary smiled her secretive little smile, the loch behind her a pool of molten oranges and purples as the huge sun set in the west and dyed the waters with its bloody hues of living fire. Then she paused, as if debating something internally, and busied herself with riddling the stove and putting in more driftwood before finally rising and pulling a slim book from the shelf. An old book in a plain cover, battered but yet intact, its yellowing pages well-thumbed by generation after generation of avid readers.

"This is *my* head, my story," she said quietly. Then

she hesitated before she continued, "And I have never shared it with anyone before. Will you read it?"

"Of course I will," I replied, meaning it, for I could see that this was not something to be taken lightly. "Give it to me, and I'll read it now, tonight."

She hesitated for one second more, one long and agonizing second, before she finally pressed it into my eager hand. *The Well of Loneliness.*

* * *

I finished that heart-breaking novel in the small hours, reading every deeply felt word as though it were a love letter to myself, aware of Mary's quiet presence in the hiss of the gaslights as she read and smoked, the little house aromatic with the sweet scent of her pungent tobacco. The fire had burned low when I finally put it down, the poignant words, *give us also the right to our existence!* echoing in my head like the desolate cry of melancholy foxes in the midnight night.

A gray sunrise was creeping cautiously from behind the distant mountains, and I could hear the first chirpings of the dawn chorus as the waves from the incoming tide lapped gently at the foreshore. I was aware of her watching me intently, fearfully, not speaking, but such a look of pleading on her face. Her beautiful, beautiful face.

"Why did you give me that to read?" I finally asked, and she looked at the bare boards of the floor for a long moment before she replied. I sat listening to the pounding of my own heart, aware that I was experiencing sensations that I had never recognized—or at least acknowledged—before. Such as my nipples being as hard as rocks inside my bra.

"Because I wanted you to read my story," she said, very quietly, her voice a low burr amid the dying embers. "And, because, I think, that you are a lot like me. Maybe, even the same as me…"

"And am I the same as you?" I asked, my body

thudding with excitement.

"Only you can know that," she replied, her breasts rising and falling with her breathing.

"But how can I tell?" I pleaded, wanting her, wanting her so badly.

"The same way you can tell if you like a book or a film or not: by diving straight in and experiencing it."

"I don't understand."

She laughed, but not unkindly, and then stood. "Kiss me, you fool," she said, in a fake romantic hero voice.

She had on a denim pinafore dress that fastened down the front in a row of silver press studs, and she ripped them open with a loud popping sound, like a hothouse palm with an explosive seed pod, and stood in the fiery light of morning like a marble statue, a flawless composition of Sapphic desire in her blue and white flowery panties and matching brassiere.

"Kiss me," she said again, but this time in her own voice. Her face pained and her tone agonized. Begging me, pleading with me.

I rose, hesitantly, painstakingly, like an old woman with brittle bones and arthritic joints, and walked slowly over to where she stood. Breathing. My legs stiff like a stilt walker's. I reached out a tentative hand to touch her, pull her close to me.

She smelt of tobacco and Avon Pretty Peach perfume. Her ringlets fragrant like dry bracken on an evening breeze.

"I've never kissed anyone before," I whispered. "I'm scared..."

"Don't be," she replied, pulling me to her, sharing the secrets and scents of her body with me as we began to meld together.

Her lips were soft on mine, like the warm down on a peach plucked straight from the tree. Her tongue was lazy and languid in my mouth, her hands insistent as she pulled me closer, her big breasts pressing into mine as she held me tightly.

"Strip me," she moaned softly into my ear. "Take off all my clothes. Rip them off me. I want to be naked against your naked body and feel the warmth of your bare skin on mine."

I remembered seeing her in her swimsuit the day before, her arms and legs tanned golden brown like unrefined sugar, and catching a glimpse of the thick dark fur under her armpit and wondering, for just one delicious second before the guilt charged in, what her cunt would be like. I so wanted to do what she asked, to pull down her flimsy hipster panties and unfasten the little blue and white bra that was doing nothing to contain her creamy white orbs, but I was too afraid and just clung to her, pulling her to me by her hips and not even daring to explore the contours of her beautiful round ass.

She laughed again and kissed my nose. Then she took charge and began to undress me. She pulled my bright yellow Jimi Hendrix t-shirt up over my head and kissed my quivering tits through my bra. She unfastened my shorts and pulled them down, taking my little white panties with them in one fluid stroke, leaving my hairy cunt all bare before her admiring gaze.

No one shaved or waxed in those days, or even trimmed, and my big fat pussy was a thick triangle of unruly light brown fur, like an untamed jungle of warm sphagnum moss all over my quivering pudenda.

"You're more beautiful than I ever dared to dream," she whispered, tracing around the large vee of my bush with one fingernail, making me goose pimple all over. "I want to just kneel down and eat you out right here…"

I groaned. I had no idea what that meant but it sounded so good. So very good. "Please," I begged her.

"Not so fast, Sporty." She laughed as she pulled me close again, her fingers on my round white bum. "I've still got a lot of clothes on…"

I so wanted to see her naked, to feel her thick black bush against mine, but I was still too frightened to act on my feelings. Sensing this, she took my hand in hers and guided it over her body, letting me read her as if she was an old bible written in Braille. I traced the slope of her back, the curve of her belly, the heat of her two very large breasts, the nipples so erect they felt as if they were erupting through the satiny fabric of her flimsy bra.

Then she slid her thumb down the waistband of her own underpants and stretched the elastic outward so that I could see down there, see the curve of her belly, white as snow in contrast to the tanned brown of her arms and legs, the trickle of hair leading down to the jungle below and a scent like nothing I had ever experienced before. Intoxicating me, overpowering me, making me her slave.

"Pull my pants down. Strip me."

As if in some other room and spying on the erotic tango being danced in our little house, I saw my hand reach out and slide her knickers down to her knees, unfasten the little pearl button at the front of her bra and watch it open like a giant shell in an undersea mermaid fantasy, her big milky breasts tumbling out, the nipples like rubber, huge dark chestnut brown aureoles like old half-crown coins.

"Now that's more like it," she moaned. She kissed me hard, ripping my bra off and sending the catch flying heaven knows where, her fingers tweaking my sugar pink nipples, bigger and harder than hers although I had tiny aureoles so pale that they hardly showed, a ring of soft golden hairs around each one. "Come on, get onto the bed. I'm so horny for you I'm already ready to come."

I let her push me onto the narrow cot and lie on top of me, parting my legs without being asked as she lay and kissed me, her thick bush hot against mine as we ground our throbbing cunts together.

"Fingers or tongues?" She gasped for breath between kissing each of my pointy tits in turn, sucking on the already swollen nipples, and making them as hard as rocks before nibbling on them gently with her teeth. "I can't wait much longer, I need to come soon."

"I don't know," I stammered, face flaming. "I've never done anything like this before."

"You mean you've never even played with your own pussy, treated yourself to a little gentle fingering?"

I shook my head. I had once slid my little finger tentatively up my own asshole in the shower and been destroyed by the guilt of how good it felt. But I had never dared to explore all the sticky sap-slick curves and wrinkles of my own fanny, never coaxed my clit up hard and rubbed it until the sensational feelings my biology text books promised washed over me.

"I'll show you," she said, clambering over me and putting her lips to my pussy and pushing her own rubyfruit jungle onto my face. "Do to me what I do to you."

Her hungry mouth was all over my thighs and pudenda, kissing my pelvis and belly, skimming my pubic hair and breathing me in. Then, she began to kiss my cunt in earnest, hot and hard, her delicate pink cat's tongue darting in and out of my slit like a hummingbird after nectar, making me feel so blissful that I was sure that I was dead and in rapture. I moaned aloud when she began to feel me with her fingers and then gently but firmly stretched my crack open so that my clit was exposed to her ministrations.

She kissed me hard, her fingers holding me splayed open like a split fig, as she began to lick and suck, lick and suck, and I could feel my very entrails winding tighter and tighter until I began to shake all over and I was suddenly screaming and thrusting my hips into her face, gripping the back of her head and trying to impale myself on her tongue.

"You have no idea how turned on I am right now." Her voice floated down to me as I held her tight and sobbed tears of pure bliss into her minge. "Your first mentor, your first girlfriend, your first orgasm."

"Is that what I am?" I asked in a small voice, intoxicating myself on her scent. "Your girlfriend? Really, truly?"

"Yes," she whispered, pulling me to her and planting small butterfly kisses on my mound. "But if you don't eat me soon I'm going to have to seriously consider looking elsewhere…"

I laughed and kissed her cunt and felt my own pussy twinge. "All right, but only if you do it to me too!"

"Glutton," she laughed, but went to work on me straight away.

I started to explore her with my lips and tongue. I ran my fingers through her thick dark curls and gently opened her hot fleshy flower, her secret pink orchid. My own fanny was tight and secret, just a mysterious dark fissure in the dense jungle of my bush until inquisitive fingers parted my slippery wet oyster to reveal the silky marzipan rose within. Mary's labia were lush and prominent, petal after crinkly petal protruding tantalizingly through her fur, pink on the outside like me, fiery reds inside when I slipped my finger in and parted her fleshy curtains. I kissed her and tasted her sweet-salt nectar, found her clit, massive and erect, and started to suck as she found mine and did the same…

* * *

And so the endless summer months wore on and our love affair just got better and better. We slept together in just one narrow bunk and made love when we woke each morning, and again under the icy water of the shower.

She would often waylay me as we did our chores and slide a furtive finger up the leg of my shorts and masturbate me hot and urgent. She would then make love to me properly with luxurious kisses as we lay in the sun after lunch, stripping off our clothes to swim naked in the warm waters of the loch before eating or fingering each other once more as we sun dried on the rocks. And again after dinner, and when we went to bed, drunk with red wine and each other's arousal.

But even perfect bliss must finally come to an end, and one gray morning I felt a chill wind blow as I turned over a new sheet on the calendar and saw October fast approaching.

"I don't want you to be with me at University," she said, out of the blue one day late in the month. "I want you to forget me and go out and live life."

"You sound like you're my granny." I tried to make light of the situation but I was very much afraid that I was being dumped.

"No, but you've fallen in love with me," she said without meeting my gaze. "And you've never had any other girls, or even any other friends—I feel as if I'm keeping you in a specimen jar for my own ends."

"What do you propose I do to remedy this?" I asked, fighting back the tears.

"I want you to go down to St Andrew's ahead of me, do the whole Freshers' Week thing alone, go to the dances, kiss strange women, fuck a man or two. Live life."

"And that's what you really want?"

"That's what I want," she said. Finality in her tone, although she was biting her tongue.

So I did as I'd been told—had a brief fling in my first week with a creamy-skinned titan redhead studying Divinity; masturbated a boy I had just met in a dark alleyway behind the Welcome Dance, and gave my virginity to a notorious tutor who specialized in the deflowering of his prettier students. I wrote screeds of love poems to a sultry American who finally put out at the Christmas dance and fucked me in her tiny room with a vibrator that ran out of battery power seconds before I climaxed, and packed my bag and went home for the festive season with my heart still belonging to Mary.

Although she never contacted me, I knew she was at her father's house, and I was anxious when I went to her family's New Year's Eve party with my parents. I saw her standing under the mistletoe by the huge fireplace, her raven hair gleaming with starbursts in Yuletide candlelight, resplendent in a floor-length crushed velvet dress in deep Lincoln green, the neck cut low, and her ample cleavage inviting.

"Oh, hello," she said when I approached her, as if I were some casual acquaintance whose name she couldn't quite recall. "I'm glad you came over. There is something I've been meaning to ask you."

"Oh," I said in a small voice, trying to be brave and hoping that I wouldn't embarrass myself and cry at the party. "What was that?"

"Well," she said, pokerfaced. "I was wondering if, you know, when you're done with all this university lark, if you would maybe… marry me? I really don't think I can live without you."

I looked at her incredulously for a long moment, the complex emotions I felt kept bottled inside me..

"No," I finally said, shaking my head, stony-faced. "Never. I can't wait that long. But we can get married tomorrow if you like!"

And we did. We most surely did.

AMELIA
CHEYENNE BLUE

When the fuel finally runs out, the engines splutter and fall into silence. Now there's only the thud of her heart in her ears, the quiet sky and its heavy-bellied white clouds. The increasing panic that had consumed her as she'd tried and failed to contact the ship, which was supposed to guide her in to land, vanishes. Amelia is calm now, with a clear-headed detachment. She's an experienced pilot; she knows how the Electra will glide, how it will swoop over the winds of the Pacific, descending, descending, until she bellies down in the ocean. Next to her, Fred the navigator whispers "Oh my God, oh sweet Jesus, save our souls" over and over, and one part of her mind thinks how predictable he is, turning religious as the plane and the sky part company and the possibility of death arises.

"Stop that," she snaps. "Look for land. Howland Island should be here, according to you."

He stares at her with wide frantic eyes, and she thinks, not for the first time, that the two of them are mismatched as pilot and navigator. She doesn't even like him much—his inane conversation irks her, as does his habit of releasing gas, blaming the altitude of flight. The thought flashes through her mind that if the Electra crashes into the ocean she might die next to this buffoon, instead of with her husband or one of her lovers. She shuts that thought out and scans the water. Howland Island is small and flat to the ocean. They could be almost on top of it and not know.

Fred is now reciting the Lord's Prayer. She flicks him an irritated glance. His eyes are closed. She shouts at him to open his goddamned eyes and *look* for land, and he might manage to put off meeting his maker for a while longer. He does as he's told, and they both search the ocean as the plane sinks lower, floating though the layers of wind and air currents, the sea below and Fred's heaven above.

They both see the island at the same moment. It's small, a tiny droplet of land in the expanse of water. It's dead ahead, and they are too high, it's too close, and she has no hope of banking or circling back to it. She has to put the plane down sharply and hope there is somewhere forgiving for the plane's resting place. Amelia adjusts the controls, the little plane shudders, responds, noses down at a steeper angle. Too sharp, she knows, but this is their only option. Her fingers are sure on the wheel. She can do it, she knows that. She sees dense green vegetation, and a flock of birds that come bursting out, startled by the silver plane above them that must look like some giant bird of prey.

There is somewhere to land. A lagoon—softest blue, shimmering aquamarine—ringed by jungle, a narrow collar of land around this jewel. She can see the lagoon is shallow—there's the lazy flap of a ray in the clear water—and she levels out the Electra so that its belly nearly skims the water. Fred is tight-knuckled beside her; no doubt he thinks he procured this miraculous island by the power of his prayer.

They are going to make it, she thinks. They're going too fast, but the water will slow them. She puts the plane's belly down. It hits the surface with a slap that jolts them in their seats. She sees white sand, and fish glimmering like precious stones. And just as she thinks it's okay, they've made it, the plane wobbles, a wingtip catches, and the Electra cartwheels. It's life in slow motion in the minutes before death. There is sky, water, sky, and things that she thought were stowed so securely in the cockpit come raining down around them. There is the flash of bright aluminum, a shower of ocean, the sound of Fred screaming, abruptly silenced. Then the plane comes to a stop right side up, and she's close enough to shore to see there are palm trees, dense vegetation, and a clatter of birds. She realizes her feet are wet—a side panel has been torn away and the Electra is sinking.

She's dazed, her head is throbbing, and there's blood on her thigh seeping through a gash in her flying suit. Amelia knows there's something she should do, but she can't get her mind to work and she can't remember what it is. But then she smells shit and looks across at Fred, at the angle of his neck so abruptly tilted, and the wires uncross in her head, and she knows she has to get out of the plane. She must save herself because it's too late for Fred.

Her body seems to work, although her left wrist hurts, and she has a headache that pounds like the big bass drum in the band that played her off in Miami on this around-the-world trip. She was to be the first woman to fly around the world, and the first person to take the longest equatorial route—those honors will go to someone new and fresh now. She unbuckles the lap strap awkwardly with her good hand, grabs the emergency kit stowed behind the seat, water bottles, her sextant, and her case of personal items. The water is up to her knees, coming in faster, and she doesn't know whether the lagoon is deep enough that the plane will sink completely. She shoves the hatch with her shoulder, and the bloom of pain in the joint brings tears to her already salty eyes. Another fierce push, and her shoulder screams in protest but the hatch opens and she tumbles out into the water.

She can't feel the bottom underneath her feet and she starts swimming awkwardly with her good arm, holding the emergency kit above her head until it penetrates her fogged brain that it's wrapped in oiled cloth and should be waterproof.

The shore isn't far away, but time feels warped, fractured, distorted, and she could be swimming for minutes or an hour. She doesn't look back at the plane until her feet catch on the sandy lagoon bed and she drags herself up the beach and turns. The plane is listing to one side, a wing and the top of the cockpit show above the water. She doesn't mourn Fred, doesn't know if she can, as it was his error, his insistence on this bearing for Howland Island that has brought her to this. But she sits on the sharp coral sand, clasps her knees, and stares out at the Electra. It doesn't sink any lower, so she may be able to swim out another day and see what she can salvage. Fred's body too. She owes him a burial, but that is all for later.

She's thinking about later, she realizes, now that death is not so imminent, she's thinking of survival. Food, water, fire. A signal fire. There will be search parties for she is Amelia Earhart: America's greatest heroine, the dashing aviatrix, the first woman to fly solo across the Atlantic, the first woman to fly above 18,000 feet, the first person to fly solo from Honolulu to Oakland. But not the first woman to fly around the world.

The dense humidity is making her headache worse. She rises to her feet and staggers in a weaving line to where the rainforest touches the sand. Before she sits, she checks herself over, running shaking hands over her body. A sore wrist (not broken), throbbing shoulder (not dislocated), a swollen knee. A pounding head and an overwhelming need to lie in the shade and sleep. She takes a careful scanty sip of water and succumbs, wondering as she does if she will wake again.

* * *

She wakes in the dark and lies still listening to the crack of branches and scuffling noises in the rainforest behind her. There are stars, great swathes of them, the same stars she's seen a thousand times from the cockpit. Her mouth is dry and tastes of salt and her short hair feels stiff under the flying helmet.

She wonders if the search parties have found the Electra yet—although how could they? She doesn't know where she is, just that it's not Howland Island and they will surely be searching around there first. Tomorrow she will light a signal fire, find food, water... She sleeps again before she can finish the thought.

* * *

The morning is bright, and she wakes blinking and disorientated. Her body hurts, each joint as stiff as rheumatism. She remembers, and bows her head in memory of Fred, of the plane, of the failed around the world attempt.

When she raises her head again, she sees someone standing, straight and tall and slender as a young palm tree. She blinks, sure she must have imagined the person, but they are still there. It is a woman, young and naked, with dusky skin and long hair tangled in a snarl over her breasts.

She rises and stands still, her palms open, facing outward to show she means no harm. "Hello," she says and her voice is a rusty croak, thick with sorrow and pain. She waits for the woman to come forward, but she remains in the same place, poised like a deer for flight.

"My name is Amelia," she says, although she guesses she won't be understood.

The other woman treads a cautious path forward. She carries a green coconut. She puts it down on the sand, and retreats step by step. Amelia sidles forward,

127

takes the nut, and steps back again. It's a stately, wary dance. "Thank you," she says.

She thinks of the coconut water inside and salivates. Her fingers fumble in the emergency kit for the knife she knows is there—surely she can slice her way through. But her wrist hurts and she drops the knife, cursing as it slips from her hand into the sand.

The other woman comes forward; there's more confidence in her step, as if she's assessed Amelia to be no threat, this fumbling person with strange clothes, and short hair like a man's. She has her own knife, and in quick, deft strokes she slices into the coconut and offers it to Amelia. Amelia takes it and gulps, aware of her parched and salty mouth, of her shaking hands. She drinks it down and her stomach rebels, and it comes straight back up in a gush of stomach acid. She sinks to the ground again, defeat and pain the twin razors in her head. But she is Amelia Earhart, and she will not be broken or beaten. There must be people here on this island, and they do not mean to harm her, not if this woman is anything to go by. She can rest and then rescue will come.

But there are no others. When she is able to walk, the woman takes her to her camp. It's at the edge of the rainforest, overlooking the lagoon. There's a smoldering campfire, a rudimentary shelter of woven palm leaves, a pile of mollusks' shells, split open and discarded, and a couple of sea turtle shells. There are some rudimentary spears, and a tattered net, oft repaired. It has the look of habitation, of a life spent here in the shade of trees, eking an existence.

Amelia looks around. "Are you alone?" she asks, although she already knows the answer. Her hand sweeps out. "Where are the others?"

The woman bows her head and kneels by the fire, coaxing it into life with a handful of dry leaf matter. Then she rises and goes to the remains of a canoe. It's battered and starting to rot in places. The woman removes the palm leaves laid carefully over the top, and Amelia sees that the canoe that once kept water out now keeps water in. The woman scoops a careful handful of water to her mouth and gestures for Amelia to do the same. She does so, careful not to drink so much that her stomach rebels again. She looks around the makeshift camp, and realizes that this woman has been alone here for a long time.

Sorrow overwhelms her. She who is so strong, so capable, so beloved by many, sinks to her knees in the damp and musty leaf litter, puts her face in her hands and cries. There are tears for Fred, for the Electra, for her husband no doubt frantic in America as news of her disappearance reaches him. There are tears too for her dream, cut short, cut down, the around the world flight that will not be hers to claim. But then she stops crying and straightens her shoulders. She ignores the throbs of pain from around her body, and rises. There is no salvation yet. But rescue will come and she will return.

* * *

The days drift by in a silent dream. Amelia and her companion communicate by gestures, although they now have names. "Amelia," she says, pointing to herself. "Amelia." But the syllables are strange, and her companion manages "Meelie", which Amelia likes as it sounds the same as her childhood nickname, and this strange and fractured interlude is like a childhood game of explorers, played with her sister. Likewise, Amelia cannot understand her companion's name. She settles on "Lae," because it sounds a bit like the port in New Guinea she'd last taken off from, and saying that name often in a day keeps her focused.

She learns by sign language that Lae had gone fishing one day from her island home, a long, long way away. She'd dropped her paddle when startled by a shark

129

under the canoe, and had been unable to retrieve it. She had drifted for a long, long time, the canoe taken by the currents. Lae had nearly died, the sun hot, with no water. She'd managed to catch fish in her net—the same net that now hung tattered but useable in their camp—and this had sustained her until the canoe washed up here, many days—weeks?—later.

At first, Amelia keeps stubbornly to her flight clothes. Wearing them is who she is, and rescue will come any day now. Any day. But she watches Lae running naked and unashamed along the shores of the lagoon, fishing from the shore with her tattered net, gutting a sea turtle and then walking thigh deep into the lagoon to clean herself. She sees Lae's menstrual blood running down her thighs, and the care with which she washes herself on those days. There are sharks in the lagoon; she sees their fins cleaving the water.

She learns that the lagoon has one opening to the sea. At low tide, she can walk across the bar and see the Electra sitting above the water. At high tide, the bar is submerged and the fish come into the warm and shallow lagoon from the sea. Then, only the cockpit and one wingtip of her plane are visible.

Amelia builds a signal fire on the western shore, figuring this is where help will come from. She goes there several times a day, standing in her stained and sweat-crusted flying suit, scanning the horizon for a ship. But none ever comes. At night, she plots her location by the stars and realizes that Fred had been wrong, so very wrong, and they are nowhere near Howland Island, but much farther south, maybe three or four hundred miles. Rescue, when it comes, will be a while longer.

She learns which shellfish are good to eat, and which fish are toxic. She learns to cast the net, to gut a sea turtle, and how to catch rainwater in the infrequent rains that fall. She learns how to defend against the giant coconut crabs, and she learns too how delicious they are to eat. As the weeks wear on, she discards her flying suit, piece by piece, the helmet first, her shoes last, until she too is naked and brown on the island.

She resists going out to the Electra at first. Rescue will come and those rescuers will take Fred's body, carry it home to America. The Electra will be salvaged. Although she will not fly again, she will be carried home by ship—the plane that nearly made it. But as the weeks wear on with no sign of rescue, she thinks more often of the parts that can be scavenged from the plane. She goes out alone one morning, swimming across the lagoon at low tide, and climbing up into the cockpit. The stench makes her gag. Fred's corpse, fast decomposing, is still in the copilot's seat. There is bone, white and eternal, showing through his face. Clamping her jaw against the stench, Amelia searches the cockpit, finding tools, a blanket—sodden, but it will dry. She pries off a curved Perspex window, some aluminum sheets from the fuselage, and tows them to shore. She returns, takes rope, more panels. She does not have the strength to do anything with Fred's body. He is heavy, and she is now whipcord from the poor diet. She doesn't know if he would float or sink or fall apart once freed from his seat, even if she is able to get him free. Better to leave him with the Electra as his coffin, better that his bones be picked white and clean by scavenging sea creatures.

She returns to shore, to Lae, who takes one look at her desolate face and comes to her and holds her. In comfort, maybe, but also in acceptance.

It's a turning point. Meelie thinks more of the island that is her home, less of rescue, less of the distant place America. The signal fire is unattended, dies down, goes out, and she does not relight it. She and Lae evolve a language of their own, part English, part the Polynesian tongue that is Lae's.

And there is more.

Lae touches her. At first in comfort, then in friendship, but now, the touches are more. There's a yearning, a wistfulness to them, as Lae's fingers stroke her hand, linger on her waist as they lean together by the fire at night. Lae's touches gain a boldness that Meelie is yet to return. It's not that she doesn't welcome the touch— she does, as love and human contact are a necessity to her, and she's always loved the physical side of love. Indeed, she and her husband had an open marriage, and her lovers were always women. But much as she wants to turn to Lae, fall into her, push her hands into Lae's salt-crusted hair, and kiss her, she resists. It feels like coercion, like all the stories she's heard of white invaders and native populations. But as the weeks move on, and Lae's touches grow more insistent, Meelie comes to the knowledge that they are not American and Native anymore, they are islanders both. This is their island, and here they are equal. If Lae wants her—and oh, how she hopes she does, that she is not misinterpreting—then it is another part of their life together.

They sleep on their bed of fronds, huddled together for warmth, the scavenged blanket from the plane underneath them. Meelie has picked apart the seams of her flying suit, spread it out so that it partially covers them, but in the cool nights they entwine, bare limbs together. Their shelter is sturdier now, and the panels from the Electra collect more rainwater in the infrequent rain that falls. They are comfortable. There is food, water, shelter, and now, maybe, love.

At night, in the dark, Lae's caresses become bolder, and her fingers more urgent. She seeks the peaks of Meelie's nipples. Her breasts are slight, skinny, like the rest of her, but her nipples are still large and dark, sensitive to touch. Lae's fingers feather over them. She pinches lightly, and Meelie jumps, but Lae's fingers are moving on, tracing her shoulder, now healed, back down over her breasts, and down to her concave stomach. The fingers hesitate and when Meelie doesn't respond, they move up again.

Meelie exhales, unaware until that moment that she had been holding her breath. She wants to kiss Lae, take her mouth, and do some explorations of her own. Her limbs feel leaden, as if pushing against water, and her hand twitches with need.

Lae takes Meelie's hand and settles it around Lae's waist. The safe zone. From here, it can be a touch of friendship or the caress of a lover.

Meelie has never been one to take the safe path.

Her fingers seek soft coffee curves that she's traced so often with her eyes. Large, dark nipples, with the wide areola, like flowers in the evening. And down deep, deeper down, to the junction between her thighs, her sex, which is dewy moist, like their jungle home after rain. She wants to taste, but in the darkness as they lie face to face, the tattered flying suit offers some protection against the rats and crabs that roam at night. So she stays, face to face, kissing, tasting, and lets her fingers explore in the damp cleft. She feels the sparse pubic hair, silken and straight, so different from her own profuse curls, and seeks within the folds to find her clit. Her pearl, as she used to say to other lovers, who preferred the softer euphemisms of female love. She's the aggressor now; Lae's fingers are stilled, clenching and unclenching on Meelie's hipbone.

Meelie strokes, coaxes, and delves deep with two fingers, always concentrating on the steady two and fro of fingers on clit. A steady pressure rub, a delicate touch, she tries them all, and is rewarded with Lae's shriek of pleasure, loud in the dark night.

When Lae's breathing has slowed again, Meelie takes her lover's hand and directs it down. Lae understands, and smiles against Meelie's lips. In the time she has been on the island, Meelie has never self-pleasured. Life was about survival, about food, water, protection, safety. So now, when Lae touches her outer lips, lightly strokes, the ripples are like sunlight finding a dark place. Her eyes widen, she sees the dark hair, the young face that is now so dear and so familiar, she sees in the moonlight Lae's the earnest desire to please, to love and be loved. Meelie surrenders to the touch, and her orgasm is as intense as any she's ever experienced. There's love and relief and yearning in the shudders, but there's also a coming home.

In the brightness of day, they do the things that all lovers do: they kiss, they murmur endearments. They wade in the lagoon, brown skins close together, and fish with the net, but the fishing stops abruptly as they run to shore to finish the loving they started in the lagoon with touches and kisses. Meelie gets to taste between Lae's legs, her sharp exhilarating taste, and from Lae's exclamation of joy realizes that she is the first person ever to taste her there.

Lae is a willing pupil too, and Meelie spreads her thighs, upturns her face and breasts to the sun, and delights in the lap of a tongue on her clit. As the aftershocks of orgasm die away, she realizes a coconut crab has entangled its pincers in Lae's hair and she leaps to her feet for the kill. It's fully two feet across and delicious eating.

As the months wear on, Meelie stops thinking about America, about the place she once called home. She stops tracing the path of birds against the blue sky, stops following their freedom with wistful eyes. And when, finally, she sees a ship out to sea, she does not run to light the signal fire. Indeed, it's a sodden mess of timber now and would not light even if she tried. Instead, she turns her back on the ocean, bows her head against the sky, and turns back to Lae.

Lae kisses her again and it's like flight.

GHOST OF SHE
JILLIAN BOYD

I looked into her eyes, and I didn't see Her.

Not the her in front of me, fingers entwined with mine and lips kissing me in the here and now, but the Her before her. The Her that had left the scar on my heart, still sore and healing. I looked into her eyes, and I didn't see Her.

But, in a way, She was always there, no matter what I did. The ghost of She Who Left. I'd tried desperately to move on with a constellation of hers, but She Who Left hung like a shadow over it all. She was there in the mornings, in the empty space in my bed. On my shoulder at work, and as I ate, showered, shaved, and shagged myself into forgetting her. In my fantasies, in between my naked thighs and on the wet folds of my cunt, her fingers ghosting their way across the span of my body in my fucked-up dreams.

Sometimes I forgot why I loved her in the first place. Considering the mere memory of her inspired such tangled feelings of hatred and sorrow, spiked like needles on a cactus; it was hard to remember why it was once different. Why her name now felt like barbs of poison in my mouth and mind.

"Are you all right?"

The light, bright voice punctuating my train of thought reminded me of the existence of the petite brunette on my lap, dress bunched under her exposed breasts. Her name lingered in the back of my mind along with the reminder that we were about to fuck in a toilet cubicle in a nightclub in Camden on a hot summer Saturday night. Our flesh was sticky, and the music banged deep through the thin walls of the bathroom. On a good day, on a *very* good day, I'd have been giving Becks—"a bit like the beer"—her third or fourth orgasm right now because, goddamnit, if she wasn't one of the most gorgeous women I'd ever laid eyes on.

But she wasn't the redemption I craved. She wasn't what I needed, because even now in this world of throbbing noise and wet arousal, I could feel Her specter like a demon on my back. And it was ever so. A vicious cycle that had spanned the better part of two years, and led me here to this club, to this woman who had a name that sounded a lot like the beer, and to the inevitable moment when I surprised myself by pulling up the straps of her dress and covering her beautiful breasts again before I asked her to get off my lap.

"What? Do you not... do you not want to anymore?"

I shook my head and my body moaned in regret as she obliged. I stood, dusted myself off, unlocked the door to the cubicle, and walked out on Becks and the club and the noise.

This time, I actually made it home before there were any tears.

* * *

It had been so much worse when She'd just left my life. I fell apart at every curve and bend. I couldn't go out, could barely sleep and eat, for what seemed like months. It was a break-up, plain and simple, in that she broke me when I least expected it and I remained broken for a very long time. Friends and family saw it coming about as much as I did, which was just south of Never Ever. She and I had been together since time immemorial, the best of friends first, then hesitant lovers as we explored this *girls being with girls* thing together. And then we were a couple. Girlfriend and girlfriend, and, secretly in my head, I longed for the day we could be Mrs. and Mrs. because that was what was going to happen. We had no obstacles left to conquer, no trials and tribulations left to face. We'd spent years and years together and we were still together, in love and lust until the end of time. What the heck could stop us?

Turns out, She could stop us.

* * *

After I'd walked out on Becks and the club and cut another line through the tangled web of reconnecting me, I did something I would have never expected: I stopped looking for sex. I stopped looking for redemption in the pussy of another woman and I tried getting on with my life.

"Try getting a notebook and writing things down," said my psychiatrist. I sighed, leaning back in the deep leather chair that I would have stolen and set up in my own house if I could. It was still hot and humid outside, even more so at midday. I was very grateful that Dr. Dubois had the air-con going in her office. If these were different times, I'd have had a fan glued to my hand.

"It doesn't have to be coherent. Just write down anything you feel and think when you feel like writing it down. It's about getting things out of your system in a creative, stimulating way. Think of it as part of the healing process."

I nodded, throat dry. "I'm not much of a writer though."

"That doesn't matter. The beauty of it is that writing skills don't come into it—although I have had a couple of people tell me that, by doing this regularly, they gained an interest in writing. Try it on for size and see if you like it. If nothing else, it will give you an outlet for your feelings when there's no-one around you can talk to."

When I finished my session with Dr. Dubois, I walked a couple of blocks down to a little stationery store and picked the first notebook that caught my eye. I didn't give it too much thought, reckoning I'd probably manage a couple of half-assed scribbles before I forgot about it. But I didn't.

It didn't take me long to make a habit out of writing stuff down. Memories of She, memories of first blossoming love, shattered hearts, and cunt lips fattening with wet arousal. Scrawls of anger, doodles, and screams into the void of lined paper. All done over a slice of carrot cake and a latte at a coffee shop near my office. It was my little ritual. My lifeline.

And a reminder that I'd forgotten just how much I loved cake.

I started spending most of my longer breaks at the coffee shop, just scribbling words and feelings down on the blank space in front of me. Enough time for my face to become recognizable to the staff, enough time for the head barista to smile and ask if I wanted *my usual* when I came in. Small kindness, but that was enough for me at the time.

And then, one weekend morning, I decided to spend my day off writing there. I didn't quite know why, but something drove me out of bed on that warm Saturday morning and down to the coffee shop, to the equally warm grin of the head barista.

"Well, well! You're practically part of the furniture by now," she said, already scrambling to get *my usual.* "Oh, wait, did you want your usual or do you want something else? We've got some gorgeous red velvet cake today—fresh cream cheese icing and all."

"I'll have a slice of that then, if you don't mind," I said, surprised to feel my lips, for a change, not stuck in a permanent expression of sadness. I was almost smiling at this woman. I realized I'd never taken a good look at her before and, as she deftly cut a thick slice of red velvet, I allowed myself a moment to check her out. Hair like a campfire flame, big bright smile, and blue eyes that could seemingly see straight into your soul.

She was kind of beautiful, really.

"Here you go. There's a nice quiet seat by the window, not too much sunlight, but enough to see what you're writing," she said, pointing toward the aforementioned seat. "I'll bring your food to you."

So she did. It wasn't until later, when I looked up and found her stealing a glance at me, that I realized the napkin underneath the plate had her phone number on it. I didn't know what to do. I didn't know how to feel, and worst of all, I didn't know how long it would take me to start feeling the specter of Her on my shoulder. The barista—Danielle—was gorgeous, no doubt about it. She was someone I could actually see myself going on a date with, and not just emptily fucking in some bathroom stall or trash can back alley.

But I couldn't help wondering if, somehow, that wasn't worse. If the potential pain from this little suggestion wasn't going to sting harder when I inevitably let her go because of Her ghost, the ghost I could not let go of no matter what I tried.

"Hi. I mean... sorry if I was a bit forward in thinking that... I mean, I don't usually slip customers my phone number, of course but..."

Danielle had suddenly materialized next to my table, face flecked with a guilt that looked kind of cute on her. "This seems a bit silly, I know. I don't even know if you like...."

"If I'm a lesbian?"

"Yeah... yeah, that."

"I am. And it's not silly."

"Good! Good, yes, very good. Only, I just realized that I also don't even know your name."

"Victoria. Vick, for short. Nice cake."

I liked the way her pink cheeks tinged a hot red. "Thank you. I... I made that one myself, actually. Glad you like it."

"It's very good. I wanted to ask how you got the icing so sweet without making it too sickly. Something I never really got the hang of."

"Oh, you bake too? Well, I'd love to give you my recipe. If you hang on, I'll go and get it."

I hesitated. I used to bake once. Before the end of Her, before everything I was came to a screeching halt, I wasn't ever out of the kitchen. We'd joke about opening a café: I'd do the cakes, She'd do the service. Work together, love together. *Love, Together.* The name of a broken dream. I hadn't baked since, and for reasons I couldn't work out, maybe something deep-rooted inside my chemical make-up, the thought of that made me intensely sad.

"No, no, it's fine," I said quickly, holding up my hands and beating myself up on the inside. "Don't feel like you have to on my behalf. Just... It's good cake. Lovely icing. Well done."

Why the hell did I add *well done*? What was this, primary school? Ten out of ten, well done, sticker from teacher?

"Let me know if you want a second slice. On the house," she said, with a wink. "And... give me a call if you want to know how to make that cream cheese icing."

That night, I actually managed to sleep through the usual static in my brain. Instead, I dreamed of... dare I? A hint of light on the horizon? Or was that just the sun softly peeking through the curtains in the early morning?

Either way, I slept through the night. And the following morning, I—hesitantly but determinedly—rang the number on the napkin.

* * *

Near the end of us, it was as if Her voice had given out. Making way for sighs and noises that sounded like the world was eroding from underneath Her. Sighs and noises that sent my heart sinking into my stomach because I couldn't understand why She wasn't speaking to me. I wanted to grab Her by the collar and demand that the words come out of hiding. I so desperately wanted to know what was going on in that butterfly mind of hers that it ate me up at night, consuming me bit by bit until I was a shell of a woman; left bereft of words by the one person I'd always trusted to speak.

Danielle, by contrast, talked. Sitting in my kitchen, cup of coffee in hand, she talked about the coffee shop, the bakery she wanted to open, the things she liked and the things she hated, customers that she adored and abhorred. I let her talk, reveling in the small things such as the cadence of her lightly Northern accent, the way her eyes lit up as she talked about little pleasures like kneading dough and the rumbling sound of a cappuccino machine, the way she curved her lips in seemingly rapturous pleasure whenever she took a sip of my coffee.

There was something unfurling inside me that I hadn't felt for such a goddamn long time—glowing, pleasant warmth in my veins and heart. The kind of warmth you'd get when you talk to someone for hours who shares a passion with you and can talk about things that seem insignificant to others but mean the world to you—like a secret language that only you can understand. Danielle was speaking my language, and it was a joy to hear.

"Do you want to try making those red velvet cakes, then? I've got the ingredients with me."

I blinked. "Really? Baking, I mean... you want to bake with me."

"Yeah, why not?" She smiled. My stomach fluttered.

"Come on, Vick. You want to know how I make my

cream cheese icing, don't you? I don't share my secret recipe with everyone."

Danielle fluttered her eyelashes in an exaggerated fashion, letting that last sentence sound like it came from a Texan Southern Belle and not from just west of Manchester. I looked at her, hand on hip like she was tutting me with her body and, out of nowhere, felt a bit ridiculous. For once, just once, I didn't want my brain to redirect my every waking thought straight back to memories of my ex. Baking was my thing. My Thing, capital M, capital T. And if Danielle was offering me the chance to have some fun—because god forbid I should have fun, right?—and bake red velvet cake with her, then I was going to damn well take it. Ex be damned.

"All right. I think my blender's in the cupboard under the stove," I said, standing up. And, to my surprise, muscle memory kicked in and coursed through my hands and fingers as I went through motions that I hadn't been through in what felt like eons. Open cupboard. Retrieve blender. Get ingredients, plug in machinery. Read recipe, and sigh... just for the sake of effect, because in reality you're chomping at the bit to get started.

Right then, Danielle went through similar motions. Danielle understood. Her mind, her fingers, and her hands understood. The thought of it sent a sudden rush of hot glowing want down my spine as I watched those fingers fidget with measures and ingredients. Fingers. Fingers ghosting down the curve of my naked body, fingers dancing between the folds of my plump, aroused cunt, fingers, fingers, fingers.

"So, what I do to the icing is just add a little bit of sugar. Not too much. And I let it set while I prepare the cake mix. When the cakes have cooled, the icing will have set enough to be nice and thick, but not thick to the point where you could club someone to an early grave with it. Creamy thick, if you know what I mean."

I smiled. "I know... I know."

* * *

Other people go to the cinema, to lunch, or to a nightclub to dance until they can't feel their feet anymore. Danielle and I, we baked. We baked up a storm from that moment on. We got to know each other over coffee and homemade shortbread. We giggled—giggled!—over more red velvet cakes, we bonded over a messy and complicated *Sachertorte* and we looked deep into each other's eyes when we were covered in white clouds of flour and creamy butter.

Sometime, one balmy evening in mid-August, while watching her heat a white chocolate ganache, I remembered what falling in love felt like—it was a lot like staring deep into the darkest abyss and finding the eyes of an angel staring back at you. In the small hours of that night I realized that I may just well be falling in love with someone again, and that it was leaving me terrified. I shook and cried into the knitted bedspread my mother had made me when I was a kid, until my mind stopped racing and the voice of Her faded away into the quiet and comforting lull of sleep.

Days later, something peculiar happened. There are moments in life where retracing your steps feels like trying to unwind a ball of string that's got no end. This was one of those moments. As I was packing my bag for work, I realized that I didn't know where my notebook was. For the life of me, I couldn't work out where, or how, I'd lost sight of it. The notebook that contained the history of me, the story of the ghost of She, the hatred, the pain, and the burning passion I'd felt. The more I thought about it, as I fidgeted with the fraying handle of my bag on the Tube, the less I could come to a logical conclusion. I'd been on work trips, jaunts to the shops, even the bloody supermarket with the notebook in my bag. The damn thing could have been left in some trash can in a hotel lobby and I wouldn't have known.

But, of course, it was simpler than I thought. Of course, I hadn't accidentally thrown it away. The truth, as it turned out from the text that materialized on my phone, was that I'd left it at the coffee shop a couple of days ago. And Danielle had found it.

The bell above the coffee shop door tinged as I walked in. It wasn't busy, but she was there, watching me approach the counter.

"Hi," I said, mentally going through everything I'd ever written in the notebook. "You found my notebook then."

"Yep."

She was angry. She was confused. She was... what was she? Was she anything? Was she what I feared or was she something I didn't expect?

Danielle leaned in to me, shutting out the world so she could whisper into my ear. "Meet me here tonight at ten. I want to show you something."

She veered back into head barista mode, asking me if I wanted *my usual*. It happened so quickly that my head felt like it was spinning right off. I didn't know, I didn't understand. But then I noticed the way she was smiling at me, eyes twinkling like little gemstones. Like she had a secret and she was bursting at the seams to share it with someone.

If I could make time move faster with my mind, I would have done anything to make ten o'clock that evening come sooner.

* * *

London, in summer, in the late evening, was a promise. A city's enticement to its inhabitants both temporary and permanent. Come out and play. The night will bring you whatever it is you want, whatever that may be.

In my case, as I shuffled around a group of hangovers-in-waiting outside All Bar One that evening, I dearly hoped the night would bring me the answers to questions I didn't dare ask out loud. Answers to Danielle, and to what it was that had nestled itself deep in my gut. Rounding up to the corner, I saw her locking up the door to the coffee shop, finishing up the late opening they had once a week. She turned and smiled at me, which made my cheeks warm.

"Hiya," she said. "Now, I'm not going to tell you where we're going yet. But I'm going to ask one thing of you."

"If it's money, I've just spent ten quid on an Oyster card top-up, so I'm out for the evening," I said, trying to keep the smile in my voice but finding it hard to restrain the creeping sense of dread snaking through me. She took my hands in hers and looked me deep in the eyes.

"I need you to trust me, Vick. Because what we're about to do might be a tad..." She bit her top lip, her eyebrows furrowing as if she was trying to think of a way to phrase it. As it turned out, there was really no other way to phrase what came out of her mouth next. "... Illegal, is what I'm saying."

I swallowed and blurted out the first—and inevitably, worst—thing that came to mind "Please don't tell me it's murder."

"What?! No! I said 'trust me,' not 'be my accomplice!' Come on, you lovely, silly person. Follow me."

We walked through the street where the City bleeds into Hoxton and Shoreditch, where stark office buildings made way for pop-up shops and street art and the sound of summer music in the air. We navigated side street after side street, and it took me a while to notice that, without me realizing it, she'd slipped her hand into mine.

Eventually, we stopped at a building that, at best, could be described as in need of a fix-up. The windows were boarded up, but in such a shoddy way that you could still see inside. Danielle was beaming from ear to ear.

"Welcome to my little secret," she said. "I... I'm not going to lie about reading what was in your notebook. I did. It was open on the table, and I glanced, and I read about... about everything, really. I hope you can forgive me. I also hope that me showing you this kind of explains that I understand what you lost."

"What is this place?"

"It's my second chance. I told you about wanting to open my own bakery. This is it, right here... come in with me."

"You want to break in? As in break the law, and trespassing, and all that sort of stuff?"

"Yeah. Hence the being kind of illegal part. Come on. I know a way in."

If she was trying to reassure me, she'd failed. But she did indeed know a way in, one that involved a lot of clambering over debris and jumping over a wall. Once inside, in the crumbling ruin of something that used to be, as Danielle said, a shop, I stood in a corner looking out over the sight in front of me. Danielle cleared a counter of dirt, and sat.

"So years ago, there was this girl, right. We met at university; she was from the States, gorgeous face, and legs that went on for days. We... well, *I* fell in love. Don't know if *she* actually did. Once we graduated, we decided to do something which, really, I should have known was a bit stupid: we set up a shop together. A bakery. It went well for about a minute. I enjoyed baking. It was the first thing I believed I was actually good at. And I loved her so much; I would have done anything for her..."

She sighed deeply, a wisp of smoky evening air dissolving in the atmosphere. "Even give her money. Gave her all my money, all my love, and probably would have given her the clothes off my back if she batted those eyelashes of hers. You can probably guess how this one ends: I lost everything and said goddamn girl got all the credit to boot. I was living on the couches of friends, on the back of the bus, or on a bench and the first night after I lost my flat, I slept in the park... Yeah, you could say I lost things as well."

And then she looked at me again, beaming like an angel. "But I found them again. A job, a passion, a life, a home... And someone who understands me. Who understands what this," she said, gesturing to the building around her, "means to me. No lies between us. This is where I want to open my second chance. And this is where I want to show you that you deserve a second chance too."

"Dani... I..."

Typical of life to throw you a curveball just when you're about to confess you're falling in love with someone. A flashing light, a *krch krch* crackle from a walkie-talkie and—Crikey!—a shadow of someone at the window. Silence, thickened by the sound of my heartbeat in my ears as Danielle leaped off the counter and grabbed my hand, pulling me around a corner, out of sight. The amber light flipped back and forth, over the scattered debris and wooden boards, illuminating thousands of tiny dust motes. But no matter how much my hands were trembling in fright, no matter how close that shadow at the window, it wasn't a patch on the overwhelming rush of sudden arousal I felt washing over me.

We were close together, packed tight against a crumbly brick wall, bodies pressed into each other. I could feel her every curve against my back, soft and warm under that slip of a t-shirt she was wearing. Sweat prickled on my skin, and I could feel my panties dampen with wetness. Was it the possibility of getting caught, trespassing here in this shell of a building in some dark side street in Haggerston? Was it Dani, and all my

149

feelings crashing into one crescendo of desperate need?

I didn't have time to think about it. Next thing I knew, Dani's hands framed my face, pulling me in for a first hesitant peck on the lips and then a full-blown orchestral rendition of a kiss that nearly knocked me off my feet. I melted into a helpless puddle as her hands slid underneath the hem of my shirt, and I moaned—moaned so deliciously because I couldn't remember the last time I'd been touched with such a sparking passion. I'd almost forgotten that my hands were itching to touch her as well, to map her every inch with fingers and mouth and tongue.

We stood there in the ruins of the past, kissing for what felt like ever and ever. She tasted of bitter coffee and sweet longing and I felt like my heart could burst.

"Dani..." I whimpered when she pulled away. She shut me up with one elegant finger on my lips.

"I want to be your second chance, Vick. And I'm going to show you just how much."

Lips replaced that finger, while her hand snaked down to the waistband of my jeans. The clink of the zip rang in my ear. The sound of a voice on a walkie-talkie in the distance. The light, soft breeze crawling over my skin, Dani worked my jeans and panties down to my ankles, urging me to stand with spread legs. Another tickle of the breeze made me aware of just how wet I was. I shivered as she looked up at me, eyes dark with lust before running first one finger, then two along my wet cleft. She moved ever closer to the swollen bud of my clitoris, her fingers dancing on hot flesh. My hips bucked, urging her to get there and get there fast.

"Please, Dani, please, please, I want... I want..."

Words fell out of me at a rate of knots. I want, I want, *I want, God, I want so badly.*

"What do you want, Vick? Do you want this?"

And then her fingers were gone, but her tongue was

there, circling and lapping at my clit. Before long, her fingers joined in again and any concern I had about anyone hearing me flew out the window along with desperate moans and cries. My hands scrambled for something, *anything* to hold on to.

"What do you want, Vick?" she said again. "Tell me what you want."

I couldn't speak. I could only live in this moment as her tongue and fingers worked my cunt and made my body hum with something more than ecstasy. Something I hadn't felt in lord knows how long. Something that I thought I'd lost when... when I'd lost Her.

And then, as I felt my body steadily grow taut with dizzying arousal under Dani's touch, the realization hit me: I would look into Dani's eyes and not see Her, because She was gone. She chose to walk away and forget, and I chose to let the thought of her linger over me like a ghost and remember.

Here in the ruins of the past, I chose, once and for all, not to give my ex that power anymore.

"What do you want, Vick?"

"Dani... Dani... Dani... Oh, god, yes!"

What I wanted was exactly what Dani proceeded to give me—an exorcism in the form of a sea of orgasms. With every lick, every stroke and every touch she set me free. My second chance... my future.

I looked into her eyes and I didn't see Her. But what I saw was so, so much better.

THE SUM OF OUR PARTS
ANDI MARQUETTE

"Would you like to start a tab?" Kim placed the tumbler on the coaster with a long-practiced flourish.

"Yes." She handed Kim a credit card. "I'm celebrating."

"This is the place to do it." Kim smiled, and went to the register to run the card. She glanced at the name. Jordan Case. With that surname, she hoped Ms. Case wasn't a lawyer. "Menu?" Kim asked as she handed the card back.

"Sure." Jordan put the card into her pocketbook. Her nails were manicured, but not painted. Kim guessed she was in her late thirties, and someone who worked in a professional environment but didn't like to draw attention to things like painted nails. Kim retrieved a menu from next to the cash register and placed it on the bar next to Jordan's drink.

"If you're not adverse to meat or total decadence, the green chile cheese smash burger is to die for. Or try some small plates, if you'd like. I'm Kim," she added. Her standard introduction, but she was a little giddy this time when she gave it.

"Thanks. I'm Jordan, by the way. But you probably knew that, from my credit card." She smiled and it lit up her eyes, a deep, warm brown.

Kim smiled back. "Can't beat a formal introduction. Let me know if you need anything."

"How about a quick history of this place? Because

the décor looks like a bordello. Not that there's anything wrong with that."

Kim laughed. "You're not far off. This saloon is representative of the era of La Doña Tules, a woman of the social elite who lived here in Santa Fe in the early-mid-1800s. She was known for her mad entrepreneurial skills and seriously ninja card-dealing skills. So she opened a gambling house down Burro Alley. We like to think we evoke her era and legend faithfully."

"That's a great story." Jordan held Kim's gaze for a long moment.

Kim wanted to say more, but another customer caught her attention. Damn. "Okay, just wave me down when you want something else."

"I will."

Kim went to take the orders from three regulars at the other end of the bar and, as she was filling a pint glass from one of the taps, she snuck another look at Jordan, hoping her gaydar still worked. She normally didn't go for blonds, but Jordan had a California outdoorsy appeal that Kim liked, and a great smile. It had been a long time since anyone had piqued her interest and the feeling was a bit of a surprise, since she hadn't thought much about dating since her mastectomy. She delivered the beer to the men at the end of the bar and went to start a tab.

"Hey, Kim."

She stopped in front of Jordan and a pleasant flush filled her torso. "Ready to order something?"

"The green chile cheeseburger thingie." She handed Kim the menu.

"Excellent choice. Fries? Or would you like me to have something healthy-looking put on the plate next to it so you don't feel totally guilty?"

Jordan smiled. "Fries are fine."

"Coming up." She went to the register to put the order in for Jordan and start the tab for the guys down the bar. She hoped Jordan was looking at her. She enjoyed how it felt, thinking about that. She turned around but Jordan was engaged with her iPad, although she pushed a strand of hair behind her ear and Kim stared at her for a moment before she left Jordan to her device and took care of a few more customers. A server brought a plate to the bar a few minutes after that. Kim took it and placed it next to Jordan.

"Your green chile cheeseburger thingie."

Jordan set her iPad aside. "It looks… big. And delicious."

Kim retrieved a couple extra napkins and a bottle of ketchup. "Holler for whatever else." She went to mix a margarita for another regular, using work as a distraction from the sparks in her chest.

"Kim," Jordan said.

"Yeah?"

"Best. Burger. Ever." Jordan held two thumbs up, which made her goofy-cute.

"Glad you like it. Hope you come back for another one." She flashed Jordan a grin, pleased at herself for the little half-flirt she'd tossed. It had been a long time since she'd felt much like doing that, too.

Thirty minutes later Jordan finished eating and started writing in a small notebook, her iPad next to her. Kim cleared the plate and napkins, thinking it was kind of cool to see someone actually writing with a pen and paper.

"Hey, is it okay if I just hang out for a while?" Jordan asked a few minutes later.

"Sure. Want another drink?"

Jordan studied her empty glass, as if deciding.

"I'll mix you something that doesn't have much alcohol. Or I can make one totally without."

"Okay. The first." Jordan handed her glass to Kim.

"I know you like bourbon. How about rum?"

"Yes. But not the over-the-top fruity kind."

"Okay. Anything you absolutely can't stand in terms of drinks?"

"Maraschino cherries."

Kim laughed. "Gotcha. No cherries." She took the empty glass and set it in the rack of dirties then mixed up a mojito in another glass. She cut back on the rum and added a jigger of ginger ale then garnished it with a strip of sugar cane and a mint sprig. "Here you go. No cherries or fruity rum."

Jordan sipped. "That is really good. Thanks."

"You bet," Kim said and went to clean up after a couple of customers. She liked that she was a little attracted to Jordan. It put a bounce in her step, a little buzz in her stomach, and both carried her through the busy evening. Once, she looked over at Jordan, ostensibly to check on her, and ran into her gaze. Jordan smiled at her and went back to writing. That added even more bounce and buzz.

By eight, things had died down and Kim started organizing and cleaning up. Jordan was still at the bar, looking up things on the iPad and sipping from her second mojito.

Kim held up a glass of Coke. "Cheers," she said.

Jordan looked up, puzzled.

"You said you were celebrating. Just joining in."

Jordan smiled and picked up her own glass.

"So what brings you to New Mexico?" Kim asked after she'd taken a drink.

"That obvious, huh?"

"I'm a bartender. I'm trained in observation."

Jordan laughed. "You were trained well. I've never been here. But I think I already like it."

"It has that effect on people. What are you celebrating?"

"I'm on a quest."

THE SUM OF OUR PARTS

Kim set her Coke down hoping Jordan wasn't one of those weird woo-woo types. "For what?"

"Not sure. I'll know when I find it."

That didn't sound as woo-woo as some. "Why New Mexico?"

"A promise I made to a friend." She set her own glass down. "And this probably sounds weird."

"Nope."

"Oh, right. You're a bartender. You've heard it all."

"I wouldn't go that far. But I have heard a lot." Kim started drying glasses from the dishwasher and setting them up for the next shift.

"Have you ever—" Jordan frowned, as if she was considering her next words. "Have you ever wanted to just say 'fuck it' and start over, but you weren't sure how to do it so you did something you've always wanted to do while you thought about that?"

Kim picked up another glass, debating how much to say. "Yep."

"Did you do it?"

"Yep." Kim looked up at her and smiled. "That's why I'm a bartender."

Jordan leaned forward and put her elbows on the bar. "What happened?"

Kim dried another glass. "I worked a high-stress job before this. Long hours, long weeks, no time for myself, but I didn't think that was important. You know. Fast-track kind of thing. Work, work, work, make a bunch of money and then work some more. I missed out on a lot of years. A lot of life, maybe."

"What was the breaking point?"

Kim set the glass down and exhaled. "Breast cancer." She looked up, expecting one of two reactions she usually got when she revealed that. Deer in the headlights expressions or the requisite "I'm sorry." Sometimes both, one after the other.

"Wow. Yeah, that would definitely make somebody stop and take stock. What kind was it?"

Kim hesitated, caught a little off-guard. "Non-invasive, fortunately."

"That's good news. What was the treatment?"

Kim dried another glass. "Mastectomy. Just one. No lymph node involvement, though they took a few anyway." She set the glass down. She sounded like the doctors who discussed the surgery results with her. "No radiation or chemo. I was lucky." She knew that now, but luck still left an uneasy shadow when she looked in a mirror.

"Did you have reconstruction?"

"No. Tired of doctors and surgery."

"How long ago was your mastectomy?"

Kim finished the last glass. "Twenty-two months, fourteen days. But who's counting?" She smiled. "So yeah, that was my breaking point." She picked up a clean cloth. "Maybe turning point's a better way to put it. Since I didn't break."

Jordan picked up her glass. "Turning point. I like that. Here's to you, and the last twenty-two months and fourteen days. And to many more days in the future."

Kim smiled. "Thanks."

Jordan set her glass down. "So you just walked away from your other job?" she asked, admiration in her expression, warmth in her eyes.

Kim stared at her, maybe a little too long. She fiddled with the towel. "Pretty much. So how about you? What are you leaving?"

"At the moment, a really shitty relationship and a crappy high-stress job."

Kim made a sympathetic noise. "Was there a turning point for you?"

Jordan grimaced. "My best friend died."

"Shit. When?"

She looked at Kim, and Kim recognized relief—the kind she herself felt when she didn't get the expected reactions to her cancer story. "Six months, five days. But who's counting, right?" She smiled, but it only lasted a couple of seconds.

"Damn. What happened?"

"Afghanistan. She was in the Army."

"Oh, hell." She heard loss in Jordan's tone.

"Right. We'd been buddies since elementary school." Jordan was quiet for a while, staring into space. She looked down, but Kim saw the tears and wished she could hug her.

"Friends like that are hard to come by. Is she the one you made that promise to?"

Jordan focused on Kim again. "Yeah. She used to come to New Mexico all the time, because she loved it here. She wanted to move here when she finished in the military. She'd try to get me to come with her, but I was always busy. Always working. So when she went to Afghanistan, she made me promise that I'd go to New Mexico, either with or without her."

Kim reached for the box of tissues she kept behind the bar and set it next to Jordan, who took one and wiped her eyes. She thought about squeezing Jordan's hand in support, but didn't.

"When she died, it made me think about a lot of things."

"I can relate. Did you quit your job?"

Jordan smiled, and this time it lingered and lit up her face. Kim tried not to stare. "Damn right I did."

"Congratulations. And hold that thought." Kim went to close out a check and get a new customer a drink. She got him change then returned to Jordan, who had closed her notebook and iPad, and it made Kim sad, because it meant she was leaving.

"And yes, I left the shitty relationship, too," Jordan

said.

"Good for you. How long were you in it?"

"Five years and change."

"But you figured it out."

"Should've listened to my friends about her. How about you? Did you leave a shitty relationship, too?"

Kim noted the pronoun. Her gaydar still worked. "It left me. About a month before I had the mastectomy."

"Shit."

"It was for the best. We didn't see eye to eye on much. I've been focused on other things since." Mostly healing in several ways, which was slow going.

"Well, like I said, here's to more days." Jordan slid off the stool and stood. "Guess I'm ready for the check."

"Sure. Hold on." Kim went to the cash register and charged one drink to the house. She brought the receipts and a pen and set them in front of Jordan, who picked up the itemized receipt and studied it.

"There's a drink missing," she said.

"That's because I bought you a drink. In honor of your quest."

"Thanks." Jordan signed the receipt. "And thanks for talking. I enjoyed it." She hesitated. "A lot." She smiled, and Kim knew she'd think about that smile and how it echoed in Jordan's eyes for a long time.

"Same here. Come back for another burger." Kim hoped she didn't sound as disappointed as she felt.

"I will. Take care." Jordan left the receipt on the bar, gathered her things, and left. Kim watched her go, the little buzz she'd had all evening fading with every one of Jordan's steps. She picked up the receipt. Jordan had left a twenty-dollar tip and a little note at the bottom, under her signature. "Catch you later!"

Kim smiled. Fun while it lasted. She went back to work.

* * *

Kim studied herself in the mirror. She was finally used to seeing her chest with one breast, twenty-two months and twenty days after the fact. Seven months ago, she'd decided on a tattoo to mark where her breast had been, and she liked how that tatt looked, the vibrant greens, yellows, blues, and reds of Quetzalcoatl, the Aztec god who sometimes took the appearance of a feathered serpent. He did on her skin, a dragon without legs whose body was a muscular, serpentine splash of life over her scar, and his tail curled up to her shoulder, while his feathered fierce head rested on her sternum, almost touching her remaining breast, across a background of glyphs from one of the god's temples.

The tattoo artist had taken several sessions to do it, given its size and color. All Kim had felt during each of them was the pressure from the tattoo gun because the mastectomy had taken nerve sensation along with breast tissue, and she was mostly numb from her armpit to an inch below her scar. The surgeon had said that would happen. She might get sensation back. She might not.

Kim pressed on her skin, and traced the lines of Quetzalcoatl's tail down to her scar, barely visible, until she found the spot where the numbness ended below it. She ran her fingertips slowly back and forth along that boundary, and wondered how another woman might see and feel her, if Kim decided to remove her shirt and allowed someone to touch her again.

She thought then about Jordan, and the little buzz she'd gotten last week. Kim liked the buzz, and she liked thinking about Jordan, but losing a breast had affected her more than she had predicted, although she'd never worn feminine-cut clothing or worked to attract a male gaze. Funny, how she carried the weight of culture, history, and womanhood somewhere in her psyche. She slipped her prosthesis—squishy silicone—into the pouch of the left-hand side of the specially-designed mastectomy bra and adjusted it before she put it on. Once on, she leaned forward and manually settled the prosthesis more naturally into place. She checked herself in the mirror, then put on her work shirt, a light blue button-up, and tucked it into her black trousers.

Twenty minutes later, she was slicing limes behind the bar while she sang a Kenny Chesney song. "A bottle of wine and two Dixie cups..." She sliced, bobbing her head in time.

"I love that song."

Kim looked up, startled that she'd been singing louder than she thought, and then grinned as Jordan took a seat at the bar. "Hey, stranger. Back for another green chile cheese burger thingie?" Her heart pounded a little harder.

"Maybe. How about one of those mojitos you made me the last time?"

"Comin' up." Kim set to work on it, stealing a couple of glances at Jordan, and her well-fitted blue tee. She'd tied her hair back and it better exposed her face. Kim's buzz returned, full-force, and she welcomed it, like an old friend.

Kim set the drink in front of Jordan with a slightly different flourish than the last time. Jordan handed her a credit card.

"Start that tab."

Kim took the card, ran it, and handed it back. "So how've you been? Find what you're looking for?"

"Maybe. I had to do a favor for my friend. Still processing."

"Ah."

"But it was good." Jordan picked up her drink and sipped. "And this is as good as I remember," she said. "I'm going to tell everybody I know to come to Santa Fe to this bar—"

"Saloon," Kim corrected as she held a pint glass under the beer tap and poured.

"That, too. Anyway, to come here and ask for you, the best bartender this side of the Pecos."

Kim laughed. "Somebody's been exploring." She set the full glass to the side and started filling another.

"Feels like it. So when is your next day off?"

Kim finished with the glass before she answered. "Tomorrow."

"Do you have plans?"

"Nothing beyond the usual." The buzz spread down her thighs.

"And what does the usual entail?"

"Sleeping in, breakfast or brunch, lots of coffee, grocery shopping, working out, a bit of cleaning. I live a very exciting life, you see. Back in a bit." She took the beer to a server at the end of the bar, enjoying the buzz that had now filled her chest and seemed to make her float back to Jordan. On the way, one of the servers gave her another order to fill.

"Is that what you do since you left your high-stress job?" Jordan asked with a little smile.

"Pretty much."

"It sounds really nice. Can I crash some of your plans?"

"Depends which ones. I'm very particular about my grocery shopping." She started to make a Moscow mule, reveling in the little flirtatious jabs between them.

"Brunch. And the coffee part."

Kim pretended to consider. "I think I can squeeze you in."

"You pick. Show me one of your favorite brunch places."

"The Zia Diner on South Guadalupe. It opens at eleven." She finished the mule and poured it into a copper mug.

"Great. And now I'm ready for a green chile cheeseburger thingie."

"Same as last time?"

"Yes."

"On the way." Kim delivered the mule to a woman a few seats down, rang it up, and entered Jordan's order. She served it when it was ready but had to deal with the Friday evening rush of customers, so the next time she talked to Jordan was when she picked up her plate.

"As good as last time?" she asked.

"Better, I think. Could be the service, though."

"We aim to please."

Jordan gave her another smile. "Guess you've got a late night tonight."

"Not too bad. Eleven. But if it's busy, I'll stick around a little longer."

"Good thing you get to sleep in tomorrow."

"Yep. Want another?" Kim motioned at Jordan's nearly empty glass. Jordan was writing again in the notebook, her iPad next to her like last time.

"One more. Then I'll be ready to go."

"Gotcha." Kim mixed another for her, poured several more beers, and prepared several pitchers of frozen margaritas before she was able to check on Jordan again. She had just finished her drink. Kim cashed her out and placed the receipts and a pen next to her on the bar. "When you're ready. I'll come back around."

A few minutes later, she saw Jordan gathering her things, so she swung by. "Thanks for stopping by," she said as she picked up the receipt copy Jordan had left.

"Wouldn't miss it. Catch you later."

Kim watched her until she was swallowed in the crowd, but the buzz didn't diminish this time. Instead, it had increased. A lot. She looked at the receipt. Twenty-dollar tip again, and a phone number at the bottom with the note, "looking forward to brunch." She grinned and entered the number into her own phone before she scratched it out on the receipt. She spent the next three hours slinging drinks and bantering with customers. When eleven rolled around, the crowd had diminished considerably, much to Kim's relief. She didn't mind staying late, but she enjoyed not staying more. She finished with her list of chores and clocked out, thinking that maybe she should have invited Jordan to brunch at her house instead.

It had been a long time since she'd invited someone over she was attracted to. She'd moved to a much smaller place after her surgery, downsizing everything, starting over in her own way. She liked that Jordan wasn't part of her past, didn't have anything to do with who she was before the mastectomy. She had no image of what Kim had looked like prior to that, and somehow, that made her feel safer about sharing parts of herself she hadn't since before the cancer. She left out the front door, glad her place was within walking distance of work.

The summer night was cool on her face, but the moon was rising, and it cast light and shadows across the rounded shapes of the adobe structures of downtown Santa Fe. Raucous laughter drifted from somewhere close and a dog barked beyond that. She lingered a few moments, enjoying the down time.

"Hey. Feel like staying up a little later?" Jordan approached, carrying a paper bag in the crook of her arm.

Kim smiled. Jordan looked good in jeans. Even in the dim light from the saloon, she could tell that. "What'd you have in mind?"

"Maybe a little moon watching. If you have a good spot in mind, I can drive."

"Where are you staying?"

"La Fonda."

Kim considered. That was near the Plaza, a few blocks away. "I live about ten minutes walking that way," she said, pointing. "And I have a great view of the sky from my courtyard."

"Courtyard? Pretty sure Santa Fe courtyard moon-watching is on my bucket list."

And although the conversation between them on the walk flowed as easily as their steps, the air between them seemed to crackle. Kim stopped at a wooden door painted turquoise set into a six-foot adobe wall. She unlocked it and allowed someone other than friends and family to enter her private space.

"Hold on. Let me get some light going." Kim plugged in the string of lights on her covered porch.

"This is amazing," Jordan said, voice soft, almost reverent. She set the bag onto the café-style table Kim used for her coffee drinking. She took a bottle of wine out of the bag and then two red solo cups.

"Dixie cups don't always hold up," she said as she unscrewed the wine's cap and poured.

"I love red solo cups," Kim said. "Best way to moon-watch."

Jordan handed her one and picked up the other. "To starting over."

"To quests." Kim gently bumped the side of her cup against Jordan's and sipped. She'd picked a crisp white, which Kim appreciated.

"Oh, wow," Jordan said as moonlight flooded the courtyard and hit the smooth, rounded walls of Kim's house. "Magical. Lauren was so right."

"Your friend?"

"Yeah." Jordan stared at the sky. "God, what is that smell? It's amazing."

"Honeysuckle. It's the vines on the back wall."

Jordan put her wine down and faced Kim. "I've never done this."

"You just did. Santa Fe courtyard moon-watching."

"No. This." And she put her hand on the back of

Kim's neck and gently pulled her face close, until her lips pressed against Kim's and heat shot up Kim's back then poured into her veins and filled every part of her skin. Jordan's other hand tangled in Kim's hair and the length of her body pressed against her and Kim wasn't self-conscious about how her prosthesis might feel to Jordan. She wrapped her free arm around Jordan's waist, mindful that she still had a cup of wine in her other hand, and pulled her closer, sinking into the way Jordan's mouth felt and into the ache and wetness between her thighs. And oh, god, it was so good, Jordan's hands in her hair, on her shoulders, across her back. Jordan pulled away after a few more minutes and took the cup out of Kim's hand and set it on the table with hers.

"Seems you've done that plenty of times," Kim said as Jordan returned to her arms.

"Not with people I barely know."

"What? We've had dinner together twice already."

Jordan laughed. "What's your last name?"

"Perez."

"Now we're even in that regard." She pulled Kim in for another kiss and it went on and on, and set more fires at Kim's core and she wasn't sure how, but somehow they ended up in the bedroom, where Jordan lit the candles on the beside tables like she'd been there before. And then she pulled Kim close again.

"Take my shirt off," she said next to Kim's ear and Kim obliged and pulled the tee carefully over Jordan's head. She tossed it onto the floor and Jordan, down to her bra and jeans, took Kim's hands and put them on her stomach, below her breasts. The warmth of her skin heated Kim's palms while the look in her eyes heated more than that.

Jordan reached for the top button on Kim's shirt and Kim froze. Jordan stopped.

"I haven't done this," Kim said.

Jordan rested her hands on Kim's shoulders. "Since your mastectomy?"

"Yeah."

"Twenty-two months and twenty days," Jordan said, and it touched Kim, that she'd kept track. "Or twenty-one, now." She smiled. "We can wait until twenty-two months and twenty-two days. I'm in town for a while."

Kim's self-consciousness melted and she pulled Jordan's hands back to her chest. Jordan undid each button slowly, taking care, staring into Kim's eyes the whole time. She brushed the shirt gently off Kim's shoulders, and Kim let it slide down her arms to the floor. Her skin prickled in the air from the open window and then prickled again as Jordan ran her fingertips down Kim's stomach. Jordan stepped back so she could undo her bra, which joined their shirts on the floor. Kim stared, certain she had never seen anything as gorgeous as Jordan's breasts, but then Jordan let her hair down and it fell around her shoulders and suddenly Kim couldn't speak. She didn't have to because Jordan kissed her again, kissed her until Kim was weak in the knees and wanted to feel much more of Jordan against her.

Kim pulled away and undid her bra before she talked herself out of it. She caught it before it fell, the weight of the prosthesis dragging it quickly downward. She set it on the chest at the foot of her bed, excruciatingly aware that the part of herself she'd kept hidden for nearly two years was fully exposed.

"Is your skin sensitive?" Jordan asked.

"I don't have much sensation where it used to be."

Jordan's fingers went unerringly to the spot just below Kim's scar where she retained feeling. "Beautiful. And the tatt's nice, too."

Kim groaned softly as Jordan's fingertips followed the lines of the feathered serpent across her pectoral to her extant breast. Jordan cupped it, and caressed Kim's nipple with her thumb, as she leaned in and kissed the scar. "So beautiful," she said before she took Kim's nipple in her mouth and Kim hissed between her teeth, dug her fingers into Jordan's back.

The rest of their clothing created a montage on the floor and Jordan took Kim to bed, where she slowly mapped the landscape of Kim's chest with her hands and lips, until every one of Kim's nerves flared in the sweat and heat that gathered between them. When Jordan entered her, she took her time, and brushed Kim's hair out of her face with her other hand before she kissed her and slid her tongue between Kim's teeth.

Kim matched Jordan's rhythm easily, tried to pull her in deeper until Kim's breath came in short gasps and pleasure washed up her thighs like waves. And just before Kim crested, Jordan shifted her position and Kim felt Jordan's lips between her legs, and then her tongue, stroking in time with the thrusts of her fingers. Kim heard herself whimper and then lost track of everything as Jordan's mouth and fingers generated an explosion within. Kim arched with its force, and fell back against the pillows, tingling and shivering.

She pulled Jordan close, held on until her breathing returned to normal, then unleashed twenty-two months and twenty-one days across the entirety of Jordan's body, until Jordan moaned and whispered for more. Kim slid her fingers into Jordan's heat, sighing like she'd just returned from a long, hard journey. Jordan matched her thrusts and caressed Kim's face, staring into her eyes until Kim heard her breath catch and Jordan clung to her, face buried against Kim's neck as she released.

They both collapsed, a comfortable tangle of sweat-slick limbs and twisted sheets. Jordan nestled against Kim and Kim relaxed into the easy connection between them, and the magic of a moonlit night.

"Thanks for inviting me over." Jordan nuzzled

Kim's neck, a sensation that was both tender and exciting.

"I'm a big fan of bucket lists."

"Good thing. I do want a change of plans, though."

"Mmm?" Kim mumbled as she kissed her.

"Brunch at your house," Jordan said against her lips.

"Deal."

And then Jordan kissed her again, long and deep, until Kim pulled away.

"How long are you in town?"

Jordan smiled. "I'm on a quest. It could take a while."

"Well, then. Here's to quests."

"And fresh starts." And as Jordan trailed her fingers across Kim's chest, and across the tattoo and down to the spot just below her scar, she knew exactly what that meant.

SOAR SPOT
ALLISON WONDERLAND

"The first time leaving may be the hardest, but so is the first blow," Lois remarks, browsing the new donations of old board games. "So if I even *think* about going back to him, you just slap me silly, you hear? And I'll do the same for you. 'Cause if first has to be the worst, it's best if it's just a one-time thing. Not that it ever is. But if there's a first time for everything, there's got to be a last time too, right? That's why going back would be a setback, a real kick in the teeth, you know? You and I, Maeve—we're going to beat the odds our first time out."

She selects *Sorry!* from the stack and shows it to me. I shake my head. She smiles apologetically and picks again. "Ha! Here's one. This one's perfect for us: *Stay Alive*, 'The Ultimate Survival Game.' We'd better follow those instructions to the letter. What else do we have? *Trouble*, *Aggravation*, *Pac-Man*. There was a *Pac-Man* board game, really? There ought to be a *Pack-Your-Bags-And-Leave-Your-Man* game. Where every girl's a winner."

I chuckle, still in mouse-mode. But Lois is a chatterbox. Now that she no longer has to keep her lips zipped like a sandwich bag, she loves putting in her two cents' worth. I, for one, hope that zipper stays unzipped for good. After all, better to have a busted zipper than a busted lip. Besides, I love listening to her. She's that perfect combination of soft-spoken and outspoken, a cross between Clair Huxtable and Mulan. Maybe one day I'll take my voice back from the villain too.

"Two can play this game," Lois declares, and joins me on the rectangular rug of squares in the children's playroom. We don't have kids, but we do have two other roommates, so when we can't sleep, which is often, we come to the safest room in the Safe House.

Another square appears on the carpet. "Remember *Pretty Pretty Princess*?" Lois asks, lovingly lifting the lid off the box.

I remember it well. A pastel hell of junky jewelry with a leper in the loot: the black ring. If you got stuck with it, you lost the game—and, apparently, your looks.

"Personally, I think the black ring should have been the crown jewel," Lois comments, handing me a pink pawn that resembles the spawn of a bowling pin and a party hat. "What's so bad about a black ring? I mean, as long as it's around your finger and not your eye. But if it is around your eye, you can always cover it, 'til he whacks the other one—"

"—and you don't dare die!"

Mangled lyrics lead to tangled limbs, and I thank heaven for small pleasures. I live for these moments, where everything's child's play and I can just liberate my laughter and sigh into her softness. All the sore spots are gone now, although it does hurt emotionally, because she's too pretty and too smart and too straight for me, not to mention too close for comfort, especially now that she's humming into my hair. The instant I identify the melody, I pretend she's serenading me. I remember the first time I heard her sing this song, five years ago, when she was onstage and I was backstage and the only thing to strike was the set.

"That's my favorite song from *Oliver*," she says. "'Where Is Love?'"

"On the boat. But I missed it."

"Me too. I guess that means we're in the same boat. Or we would be if we hadn't missed it."

In her arms, I'm reminded of the way Snoopy hugs Woodstock, except I don't feel small at all, just hugely important. Even so, I let go, so that I won't let on that I have feelings for her. We may have met in a past life, but we've really only known each other a couple of months, and in another month we won't even be living here together anymore, so why keep in touch when we probably won't even stay in contact? And of course I'm falling for her only because she's the first woman to give me shelter from the norm. Being with Lois is completely painless. It doesn't hurt that she always has a sweet heart and a kind word and a heroic smile.

I love it when she shares that smile with me, and she probably still would be if I hadn't pulled away so quickly, like The Artful Dodger fleeing the scene after picking a pocket. Flicking the game's plastic spinner, I watch as the little gray arrow goes into a graceless pirouette. It looks as dizzy as I feel.

When the spinner stops, it points to Lois. Or to number three.

"I'd do anything to do that show," Lois murmurs, her fingers tightening around the wooden leg of the child-size chair next to her. "I know the plot is very… funereal, but hey, so was my marriage. Right after we got married, he told me I had to retire from the stage. I wasn't even professional. I was doing community theatre—for kicks. Well, those came later, but anyway… When we were dating, he was my number one fan: came to all my shows, clapped like crazy, showered me with flowers. You met him once, didn't you?" Yes, the displeasure was all mine. "But once we tied the knot, he decided he couldn't have some drama queen upstaging him; all the time I'd spend at rehearsal would be better spent with him and I had better spend it with him if I know what's good for me. Oh, and let's not forget how much gratitude I owe him for protecting me from the humiliation I was doomed to suffer as a 'hacktress' who can't hack it, especially when it comes to kissing, but what director would be dumb enough to put me in a play, let alone a kissing scene?"

She flicks the spinner with a combination of force and remorse, and I watch as it revolves in revolt.

"The first time he told me I had to give up my passion, I thought he was joking. So I laughed and launched into the Lucy Ricardo act, begging and pleading with him to let me perform, and he… well, he cut me off. Clearly, he wasn't pulling my leg; he was taking a page from the stage and threatening to break it. And that is one cast I did not want to be in. Speaking of one…" She points to the arrow, which points at the aforementioned number. "Figures," she scoffs. "He always pronounced my name funny, put a T at the end of it, so that it sounded like Lowest." She shakes her head, smiles in that woeful way that really isn't a smile at all—a wordless oxymoron. "You got a three," she says. "You go first."

I spin again, then push my pawn forward four spaces, whereupon I am instructed to beautify myself with a single earring. Just call me Boi George Michael.

Lois smirks at the perky pink plastic pinching my earlobe. "Hurrah, She-Ra!" she quips, and dips into the jewelry box once the spinner stops.

"Who's She-Ra?"

"The Princess of Power," Lois answers, as she adorns her neck with a gaudy yellow garnish. "That title rightfully belongs to my second favorite orphan, the jaunty Miss Brewster. Punky Power was infinitely more accessible—and accessorized. I would sing the theme song all the time when he wasn't around. God, I sang everything. No reason to confine myself; that was his job. Then one day I realized: I know why the caged bird sings. She's a Maya Ange-loser."

"What is she now?"

Lois smiles. It's authentic, audacious, authoritative. "Now she is a monarch in the making," she declares, gesturing to the cluster of luster-less baubles and the sliver of a silver crown. "Just call me Madame Butterfly."

"Is that a musical?"

"It's an opera. I can't sing opera. I probably can't even sing well enough to get in to *Oliver*. My husband was quite the dickens, but I'm no Nancy."

"You're not a gay boy?" I tease, because her confidence was there a second ago, and it'll be back soon enough.

Lois laughs. "Nancy—Bill Sikes's girlfriend," she says. "He's the one who knocks her around and eventually knocks her off. Now *that's* the Bill to kill." Lois nods emphatically, looking at once hateful that it happened to Nancy and grateful that it didn't happen to her.

"You could've been talking about Nancy McKeon, from that movie *A Cry for Help*. I don't know if you've seen it."

"Made-for-TV DV? I think I've seen every movie ever made about spousal abuse. Is that strange? That I'm so… interested in intimate partner violence? God, what a weird phrase. It makes it sound sexy or consensual or something similarly creepy. But I watch it and think: hey, that's me. Then, the next minute: that poor woman—that would never happen to me. But I… for lack of a better word, like *A Cry for Help*."

"We watched that movie together once, me and my… intimately violent partner," I share, taking my third turn. "It was three days after… the first time it happened. We were watching it and my… violently intimate partner kept commenting on how attractive Nancy is, as if battered women are… you know, like that's a type that someone has, no different than liking brunettes more than blondes. And we held hands the whole time. Or, well, my hand was held. Tight. I just kind of let it be taken hold of."

"Now *there's* a man who knows how to add insult to injury," Lois remarks, and I don't correct her. "Looks like Charles Dickens got it wrong," she continues, untangling a beaded bracelet from the clot. "Oliver's not the one who's twisted. Your ex is. Hey, isn't she some sort of lesbian icon?"

"My ex?" I ask, before I can think better of it, which I would have been able to do if I hadn't been so busy fastening the bracelet around the sickeningly soft skin of her wrist. "I—I mean... who?"

"Nancy McKeon."

"Oh, um, I guess she is. To some people. Lesbian people." I wonder if my face is as red as Lois's lips, which, queerly, are twisted into a smirk.

"I liked her on *The Facts of Life*," Lois shares, and I miraculously manage to steady my hand long enough to flick the spinner on the first try. "I remember she punched Blair once. I don't think it qualifies as relationship violence though, since it was only the one time, not an established pattern, as the counselors call it. Then at the end of the episode Jo owned up to it and promised Blair she'd never hit her again. And she didn't. She kept her promise. Blair forgave her. And Jo never laid a hand on her again. Not in a harmful way, anyway. I'm sure the next time she laid a hand on her, she was much more gentle. Right, Maeve?" Lois winks at me.

My thoughts are a clot of knots, just like the jewelry, and all I can do is stare at the game board and wonder if the other pink earring is going to come out before I do or after.

When she doesn't get an answer, Lois keeps talking, which she does with any subject, but this is one I almost wish she'd change. "My husband rode a motorcycle—like Jo, you know? But one day he got a car. I think he thought we were going to start a family or something. I did consider faking a pregnancy at one point, hoping that might be a deterrent, but then I remembered all those movies and how it tends to have the opposite effect, so I scrapped that idea. Anyway, on our first drive, he was at the wheel, and he made me ride in the backseat, like some sort of hitchhiking Little Miss Daisy. He made some crack about me cruising for a bruising, and in my head I talked back and said, 'I know why you got a Cadillac: you're a cad.' It was such a lame insult, but it felt good to think bad about him. I did like the car better than the motorcycle though, because I could put some distance between us."

Like I'm doing, by not being completely honest with Lois, except this distance is much less desirable. It's funny—I might not talk much, but when I do, I can only talk about the stuff that's hardest to talk about. Like how my partner played baseball: batterer up, three strikes I'm out. Like how I consider what she did substance abuse, because she made me feel insubstantial. Like how she had a beef with me every single night about every single thing, and how that beef was usually in the form of a knuckle sandwich. Actually, some good came out of each feud, glorious feud, because now Lois and I have an inside joke—*Grief: it's what's for dinner.*

"Did you ever think about doing him in?" Lois asks, and now I'm starting to think she can tell there's something I can't tell her. I'm pretty sure she stressed the pronoun too; in my mind I see it slanted: italicized and ostracized.

"I certainly thought about getting trigger-happy," Lois shares. "Emphasis on happy." She emancipates a yellow earring from the wreckage. "I used to fantasize about it when we were… well, when he was… Anyway, I had my whole defense worked out and everything." She clears her throat, and when she starts up again, she sounds like a cross between that famished foundling she'd grown so fond of and Adelaide from *Guys and Dolls*. "'Well, naturally, Your Honor, I couldn't leave him, so he had to go. So, when the opportunity presented itself, I... well, you know what they say: you got to strike while the iron is hot. Lord knows he did.'"

She clears her throat again, and now she's back to normal. "I probably could've gotten away with it. Wouldn't be my first time doing the *Cell Block Tango*. Granted, I've only committed a murder but not a crime onstage, but if I did do it offstage, it's not like I'd be taking a life. I'd be taking a life back. Plus, we dykes still get accused of male bashing. Why not broaden the interpretation and really give 'em grist for their rumor mill?"

I look at her like she's one trinket short of a complete set, which, incidentally, she is. "We dykes?"

Lois chuckles. "Well, when you put it like that, it sounds like a toy line: Wee Dykes."

"So you're a... lesbian?"

"I can be," she says, and I see her spine stiffen, but not with dread or cold or tension. No, this rigidity is mettle in its finest fettle. "I didn't think I should be, so I wasn't. But now I am." She smiles, blushing like a princess bride. "I should have just become a nun, like Jo wanted to, so she wouldn't have to deal with all the lovely lesbian lust she was feeling for Blair. Of course they couldn't address that on the show, but it's there if you watch it right. Man, that episode really packed a punch—in more gays than one." She lifts her hand to my face. I expect to recoil but don't. Instead, instinctively, I'm receptive to her touch. "You really had no idea about me?"

I shake my head, which is about as empty as Oliver's belly. "This is the first I've heard of it."

"Want to know where love is?" Lois asks. She takes

my hand. Her grip is somewhere between loose and lifeline. "It's here, it's queer, and we're going to get used to it."

Lois fishes the black ring out of the jewelry box and puts it on the proper finger. It's a tight fit, but it doesn't hurt.

I stare at the gewgaw in awe. "Does this mean I win, lose, or—"

"Draw the curtain."

"Huh?"

"I think we're finished playing," she says, and part of me wants to trust her but doesn't, while the other part of me trusts her but doesn't want to.

I can't help reviewing the situation. What if she's just trying to make up for years of inappropriate and insufficient intimacy? Or turning to a woman because she's had a terrible experience with a man? I guess, by that logic, I should have been scared straight. And I wasn't. But what if—

Lois kisses me, successfully subduing my skepticism. My heart is the first to absorb the feeling. Her kiss teems with tenderness, gleams with triumph. Puts the sensual in consensual. Her lips, watercolor-red and painting over my pain, are softer than any pillow I've ever cried into.

Stress and Distress come out for the curtain call, followed by Pain, Insecurity, Humiliation, and, finally, saving the worst for last, Fear.

I take my first breath.

Lois looks at me. There's nothing intimidating or eviscerating in her gaze. My ex's eyes were the color of Oscar the Grouch. But Lois's green isn't mean. Her eyes remind me of the Statue of Liberty.

"Did you get a kick out of that?" she asks.

"I'd better not," I answer.

Lois laughs. There's something inescapable about her laughter. This must be what survival sounds like. I guess what they say really is true: the best things in life are free.

My eyes feel damp. It's the first time I've ever cried because I wanted to, not because I had to.

Lois flips the drips off her thumbs. "Maeve, teardrops are only desirable if they're diamonds, okay?"

She's right. I make short work of the waterworks and remind myself that I am the Princess of Power, not the Princess of Wails.

When Lois touches me again, it's below the neck but above the waist. The grip she's got on my arms is neither tightening nor frightening. It's just right. Right where I want her.

When she leans in for another kiss, she doesn't have to twist my arm.

When she demonstrates her desire, she doesn't pull any punches.

When she acts on her ardor, she hits her stride.

The overture segues into the first act of love. It's a love adorned with artificial accessories. But it's also a love decked out in genuine gentleness and authentic affection.

I put it in my heart for safekeeping.

At the top of the show, I had stage fright. Now this princess is playing opposite a drama queen. Casting my nerves aside, I direct my hand to cross downstage.

Then I join her in the wings. Lois may no longer be a soft touch, but she certainly has a soft touch, and I hope she has the same sentiment about mine. My fingers feel her sex, contoured like a theatre curtain and projecting considerable stage presence.

For the first time, I don't have to chew the scenery—or, as a distraction, the inside of my cheek. I can throw myself into the role of lover and know that I bring something valuable, something invaluable, to the part. There will be no heckling, no exiting, no upstaging. Our roles are equally important.

We support one another, exhort each other to sit back, relax, and enjoy the show of hands, respect, appreciation.

Our movements, formerly curtailed and controlled, are currently agile and fragile, cautious and careless.

I hear something. It's coming from Lois, and Lois is coming. She isn't moaning though; she's murmuring—the lyrics to "I'd Do Anything," another sappy but snappy song from *Oliver*, and I hope we're going to Twist the night away.

My own finale approaches, but unlike the Widow Corney, I shall not scream, because there's no pain, only gain.

Afterward, we sit in a safe, soundless snuggle and breathe easy. It's easy to breathe when the scent is so savory. My ex smelled like wet construction paper. Lois smells like ginger and grapefruit.

She curls closer then, and I can't help but wonder if she's bothered by my body, which is shaped like a sacked potato. Or, no, a socked one. But why would she be? I am no sad sack. And I don't have scars on my body either. I have souvenirs of survival.

I gaze at the bevy of butterflies that have colonized the playroom's wallpaper. *Leave or fly trying*, I think, but I don't say it out loud because we got the message already. Loud and queer. Our first time out.

Unlike Fagin's gang, we won't be back soon. Or ever. Not when there's a fine life to be had.

"Consider yourself a winner, Pretty Powerful Princess," Lois whispers, and I don't question or quibble with that characterization.

"Okay, Miss Oliver Twist of Fate," I reply, and Lois gives me the smile for which I'd do anything. "But only because you consider yourself one of us."

S E A
ROSIE BOWER

"Is this your first time?"

Tara turned around with a start. At any other time, in any other place, she could hardly have failed to notice the woman standing beside her. She was tall and willowy, with a riotous abundance of auburn hair that belied the spartan lines of her body.

In any other place, at any other time, Tara would have spoken first. Not some trite chat-up line, but still an unmistakable invitation, each word wrapped in an unspoken desire, which demanded reciprocity. Now though, the sound of surf was so loud in her ears she could barely hear the woman's words, and her fingers itched to bury themselves, not in that windswept mass of curls, but in the sand, which caressed her feet.

"I'll take that as a yes."

Tara realized she hadn't responded. Thankfully, the woman didn't seem annoyed; there was humor in her voice, a trace of understanding.

"Yes," Tara said, belatedly, "this is the first time I've seen the sea."

That was a lie, of course. She had *seen* the sea a thousand times: in films and on television, in glossy magazines, and travel brochures. She had known what to expect. In fact, half the reason she hadn't visited the ocean before now was that she had deemed it unnecessary—she'd had a surfeit of sea, growing up. The endless expanses of water depicted on a thousand and one screens had seemed to mock her, and her parched and sun-baked childhood. Instead, she had embraced her natural habitat, had journeyed to desert and savanna and steppe, and never once looked down to the sea, miles below, as she flew from continent to continent.

Those wild, stubborn places called to her more than rolling tides and the gentle shush of foam. What could any beach tell her of sand when she had held the Sahara between her toes? Who could love the cruelty of water that was both endless and undrinkable? Surely, the most meager of desert oases held more of the true spirit of water than the greatest ocean.

Still, finally she had been caught, lured, and reeled in like a fish. Not by the pure white sand and crystalline waters of myth, but by this study in monochrome: gray sea, gray sand, gray sky. The woman's red hair was the only spot of color in sight, and it whipped around her head like flame in the brisk wind. Cliffs towered overhead, hiding her adultery from the jealous sun. She was a child of the desert and knew she did not belong here, and yet...

"Nerine," the woman said.

Tara dragged herself back from reflection, knowing that if she didn't, some future self, incapable of recalling the truth of this moment, just as one can never truly remember transcendent pain or overwhelming pleasure, would feel regret at the missed opportunity, and wonder at her reasons for missing it.

Nerine, she thought, *means sea nymph.* She wondered if Nerine would sing to her as she drowned. Or was that sirens? All the sea's denizens were equally threatening to Tara in their unfamiliarity.

"Tara." The wind whisked her voice away, stealing it and returning it to her transformed. *Terra,* the wind breathed back at her, *earth,* and she could not deny its understanding of her essential nature. She wondered if

Nerine would hear the truth the wind had found in her name. Wondered if Nerine's own name held the same prescience, and whether she should be afraid, for the sea always won in the end, its patience greater even than the patience of stone.

"I envy you, you know."

"Me?"

"I grew up here, with the sea. It was always as much a part of me as my bones. I'll never know what it's like to see it for the first time."

"I thought there never would be a first time. I intended to live my whole life and die without seeing the sea."

Tara didn't know why she told her companion this. Although true, it was a statement that had been met with disbelief, even rancor in the past, and that was from people who were not a part of the ocean as Nerine was, and had no personal stake in defending it.

It didn't occur to Tara to question the fact that the sea was just as much a part of Nerine as the arid plains were a part of her. She wondered if this flame-haired sea-witch felt ocean spray on her face at night as she slept, just as Tara, in occasional quiet moments, felt the harsh, dry breath of the desert on her skin even when she was miles away from the sand and the scrub, even when she was surrounded by concrete and only dreaming of open skies. Some understanding passed between them, and Tara knew Nerine would never ask—nor ever need to ask—why Tara had been deaf to the call of the sea for so long.

"What changed?"

"I met a man," Tara confessed, "a man who smelled of the sea." She closed her eyes, remembering. "He had grown up a fisherman, and never wanted any other life, until he fell overboard one day and tangled in the nets. He was dragged for miles behind his ship, bound and half-drowning.

"By the time I met him, he had put half a continent between himself and the ocean and it wasn't enough. She hunted him, the sea, she *haunted* him. When I knew him, he made his living gutting fish, and to see him wield a blade, you'd think it was the sea herself he struck. He smelled of brine and death, and when he cried he would taste the salt of his tears, and cry harder for they tasted of everything he had lost."

"Did you love him?"

"No more than I could love any man—it would be like trying to love the moon. We were different creatures, he and I. Different species. I bought fish from him a few times, though I don't normally care for it. I would eat it and try to taste in it whatever it was he tasted.

"I never did, but somehow it feels as though a stray bone has caught in my chest, or perhaps it is a hook lodged in the ventricles of my heart. I allowed the sea into myself, and now she insists on returning the favor."

"So here you are."

"Here I am."

"Tell me what you see." It was half-command, half-plea, and yet held a certainty that Tara would do as she was asked. "Let me see it through your eyes."

Nerine was no longer at her side. Tara felt a heat against her back, breath on her neck, but didn't turn. Nerine was as much a part of the landscape as the tide, and as inescapable—not that she wanted to escape.

"I was in a blizzard once," Tara began, her eyes on the waves and her voice as soft as the rush of foam on sand. She felt Nerine's hands snake around her sides. "The ground was white, and the sky was white. Even the air all around me was white. The snow was so thick I couldn't even see my hand in front of my face, but I knew that if I could it would have been white as well— the color leached from it until I became a part of the snow and ice."

Tara felt Nerine's hands on her chest, slowly unfastening the buttons of her shirt. The hands were cool and rough, almost indistinguishable from the salt spray that lashed at them.

"This is almost like that. It's hard, here, to pick out the point where sand turns to sea turns to sky, and yet this is so very different as well. The blizzard was close, smothering, almost, in its affection. It wrapped me in a blanket of snow, but if the sea takes me to her bosom, it will be different. She will seize me a fragment at a time, stealing me away, the same as she wears away the cliffs."

Tara's buttons were undone now, and when her shirt fell and her bra with it, she wasn't certain whether it was Nerine's hands or the wind's deft fingers that plucked it from her shoulders. The skin of her breasts and belly prickled at the sudden chill, water droplets landing like a thousand icy kisses on her flesh. She shivered, and felt bare skin against her own. When had Nerine undressed?

"Go on." Nerine's breath felt obscenely hot on Tara's skin. Tara didn't consider her words; she just allowed them to pour from her, like a river running into the sea.

"I think the sea must hold a thousand secrets, a million, and her secrets must be the cruelest of all. The desert is not kind: it will take you, skin you, flay the flesh from your bones, and leave you bleached and naked to rest under the sun. The sea, though, she is crueler still. She will devour you whole and swallow you down into the depths of her until even the sun cannot find you. What the sea takes, she holds and will not share."

Her skirt was pooled around her feet now, and Tara hadn't even felt it happen. Perhaps she already belonged to the sea, these last thoughts like the final bubbles of air escaping from drowning lungs. Was Nerine even real?

Tara struggled to remember the long limbs and bright hair of her sea-priestess, but her mind could hold nothing but sea and sky, and the lonely cries of birds. Thought trickled from her mind like water escaping between the fingers of cupped hands, and she knew that the harder she grasped at it the faster it would pour away.

She licked her lips and tasted salt, tasted sweat and sex and tears, and something else. Something indefinably other.

"*More*," breathed the woman at her back, little more than the voice of the wind in her ears.

"You look at the pictures," Tara continued, her words a tithe to the sea, "and think you understand. Perhaps you can be forgiven for that—some things are so great, so terrible, that even awareness of their incomprehensibility is huge enough to defy comprehension. You look at the pictures, and the sea is flat and clear as a garden pond, and you're tricked into believing that the difference is only in quantity. But the sea is truly alien, no more a cousin to that pond than the sun is to the tiny light you keep beside your bed to drive away the night terrors. They say we know more about the moon than we do the sea, and it isn't until you're here that you know in your heart how true that is."

Her underwear joined her skirt on the sand and she was naked, as naked as the crabbed trees that clung improbably to the cliffs above, reaching with bare, twisted branches for the sky. Tara wondered why they grasped for the sunlight with such senseless determination—they must know the sea would have them in the end.

There was a slight pressure at her back and she yielded and walked forward, one step after the other until she stood at the point where the sea touched the sand, the water kissing the tips of her toes at the furthest reaches of each wave.

"The tide is coming in," Nerine said. "It will steal the sand from under you if you stand and let it. I've seen a thousand try to wait out the tide. The sea isn't deep enough here to make it dangerous, even with your feet sinking grain by grain into the sand, but still no one succeeds, no one but me. I sometimes wonder whether they simply lack the patience, or whether the sensation of the earth dissolving beneath them disturbs them on some visceral level."

And you? Tara wondered, *is the land so alien to you that you do not fear its abandonment?* But Tara didn't ask; she didn't need to, for she knew then that, like Nerine, she would outlast the tide. She would not run—her fishmonger had taught her the folly of fleeing the sea. Its taste was on her lips now, like a lover, and leaving would not put it aside. She had a vision of all the rivers in the world running backward along their courses, the sea reaching salt-sharp fingers inland until it found her.

"Will you wait with me?"

"Of course."

Nerine's hands were cool, but this didn't bother Tara, for her own skin was just as cold to the touch, its heat leached away by the wind. Despite that, there was fire within her. She was a mountain, hot lava birthed into cold sea, and the chill could not touch her blazing core. The wind died down for a second, and that heat surged up within her skin. She felt flushed and intemperate without the breeze to cool her, and could barely stand her own stillness, but the sensation quickly passed as the wind returned to lap at her flesh with tongues of soothing ice.

Nerine's hands were cool, but her mouth was hot where she kissed Tara's neck, lips parting to expose a furnace-like heat. Tara's skin rippled, a shiver born not of cold but of desire. She wanted to turn, to return Nerine's embrace, but her feet felt trapped. Already she was sinking into the sand, particles dusting her toes as her feet began to disappear. The tide had risen noticeably now; the water, which had barely lapped at her toes, now refused to let them go. Each ebbing wave exposed less of them than the one before, and she knew that before long they would be submerged completely.

Nerine's hands on her hips kept her grounded, even as clouds boiled in the sky, and the sea ate the land, and all that had seemed certain and safe became untrustworthy. Immobilized by the tide, able only to be touched, not to touch, Tara gave herself over to the sea, and to the sky, and to Nerine's cool hands and warm mouth.

Nerine's kisses became less gentle. A hint of teeth, a sensation that mirrored the waves sucking at her feet. Tara felt as though she was being devoured, as though Nerine were nothing more than a vessel for the power of the ocean, and together they would nibble away at her, top and tail, until they met at her center. Nerine's hands stroked her skin with the rhythm of the tide, finding the crest of a wave in the swell of her hips, a cove in the curve of her waist. She ran idle fingers over the promontory of Tara's breasts and down the ripples of her spine.

Nerine's bright hair tumbled over Tara's shoulder, and she couldn't help herself, she turned her head, breathing the sea air through the warmth of those curls, feeling them trace paths across her face; runes written in an arcane tongue. They stayed that way until Tara felt as though she were drowning, and shook herself free.

Nerine's hands remained on her body, always moving, touching her with the same unfocused attention as the sea itself, which crept beneath the arches of her feet, and insinuated itself into the spaces between her toes. Nerine's hands seemed as fascinated with the muscles of her arms as they were with her breasts; they circled her navel as avidly as they rounded her nipples. Tara thought that it ought to feel impersonal, but it didn't. The attraction of those parts of her which held an inevitable magnetism to her previous lovers—breasts, buttocks, and cunt—were not lessened by this, rather the rest of her was embodied with the same allure.

Tara's arousal built slowly, rising as interminably, yet inexorably, as the tide. By the time she was writhing and arching under Nerine's hands, her planted feet the only part of her not dancing to the tune Nerine's fingers played across her body, the sea had lapped its way up her calves, swallowed her knees, and begun to swirl around her thighs. Though, flexing her toes within their prison of sand and surf, she found herself wondering how many inches of the sea's claim on her were due to the rising of the tide, and how many were her own sinking. It was hard to tell in the endless ebb and flow of the waters just how deeply her feet were buried, but she could still feel the tide stealing the ground from under her, a grain at a time.

"The tide is almost at its peak," Nerine whispered in her ear. They were the first words either had said in some time. Tara thought she made some sound of recognition in response, but it was stolen so quickly by the wind, that she couldn't be sure.

Nerine's attentions grew more focused, more precise, her intent clear. As if that maybe-sound had opened the floodgates, Tara began responding to Nerine's touch with sighs and moans that blended perfectly with the sounds of this liminal landscape. Her intake of breath could have been nothing more than the hiss of foam, her keening, the cries of sea birds. Nerine was sculpting her, kneading her flesh until she fit perfectly here, as much a part of this world as Nerine herself.

Nerine's right hand was between Tara's legs now, her left twisted in Tara's hair, holding her body straight and taut. Tara felt as though her spine was a cord strung between the two hands, which thrummed with pitch-perfect tension at Nerine's touch.

Then Nerine entered her, those deft fingers exploring her inner spaces as thoroughly as they had mapped her skin. Tara felt as though the whole of her dwelled within Nerine's hands; Nerine's fingers inside her, beckoning, her thumb on Tara's clitoris, and her broad palm cool against the heat of Tara's vulva.

Tara was sure the tide must be at its peak now, for the waters had risen until the waves splashed against her hips. Nerine's hands were so cold they were almost impossible to distinguish from the water itself, as though the sea were reaching around her and into her with fingers of crystalline ice. The fingers inside her coaxed, beckoned, and she pictured all the oceans of the world pouring into her, filling her up.

She climaxed, shuddering under Nerine's hands, fluid rushing from her in a flood to mingle with the salt sea. When the waves that claimed her finally stilled, she felt waterlogged and limp. She laid her head back on Nerine's shoulder, Nerine's arms strong and warm around her.

They stood, entwined, until the ocean abandoned them, flowing off to some other place. Perhaps it had other lovers, in other lands, who even now stood on the sand to await the arrival of their beloved. Tara pulled her feet from the sand, pausing a moment to stare at the twin craters she left behind as water began to seep up within them. They would be gone in minutes, for the sea's memory was as brief as its love was vast, but she would remember it always.

"You're cold," Nerine said, her words knowing and gentle, "and my house is nearby. Will you come home with me?"

Tara turned to take Nerine's hand, and found that she was not dismayed to discover that their clothes had been swept away on the tide. Bedecked in glistening beads of water and the salt crystals left behind as the sea dried on their skin, she did not feel naked as they crept away together through the deepening twilight, the crash of the waves a distant farewell in her ears.

DISSOLVING
CELA WINTER

"Dee? Are you asleep?"

"Mmmm?" I nearly am, spooned around Ellie with the grassy henna scent of her hair filling my head.

"Can we talk for a few minutes?"

"Uh, sure, babe." Maybe this will be quick. "'S on your mind?"

"You know how we always said we'd be honest with each other?"

That wakes me right up. I reach across her for the bedside lamp, but she stops me with a hand on my wrist.

"Leave it. In the dark might be easier."

"Uh-oh." It's a knee-jerk response, yeah, but is any other kind possible to something like that?

"Not an 'uh-oh.'" There's a smile in her voice. "It's just... we haven't been together very long, Dee, and there are things you don't know about me. Yet."

Another uh-oh. All kinds of ideas start circling in my brain, mental noise I try to squelch as Ellie, the woman I love, the woman I'm *serious* about, continues.

"It took me a while to find myself sexually. I've told you some of that."

I nod—not everyone is born knowing as I was—then remember it's dark. "Yes?" It sounds tentative, almost a squeak. I clear my throat and repeat, "Yes," more firmly.

"So anyway, I did some experimenting and, um, found out that I like, um, certain activities."

"What kind of activ—you mean like kinky stuff?"

"Some people might call it that. Think of it as... playing."

A memory surfaces, something I didn't attach much importance to at the time, of Ellie looking in the mirror, examining a bite mark I'd left on her shoulder. It was an accident, of course. We'd been doing it doggy-style and I was overwhelmed by the way she opened to me, urging me on with pleas for more. I never realized I was biting until I came down from a thunderous orgasm.

Horrified, I apologized, kissing the spot and wincing at the bruise spreading from the red teeth marks. She told me not to worry, that it was a thrill when I got so carried away. I thought she was just being brave. Looking back, could it be that she was, maybe, admiring the bite? That it turned her on? She did drag me back to bed very shortly. I hadn't made a connection until now.

"Do I have to hurt you?" The way I still feel over the biting thing, I'm not sure I'm up for that.

"No." The smile voice is back. "And I won't hurt you, unless you want me to."

That answers my next question, but, "Are you saying that you, uh, we aren't—? I mean, that I don't—?"

"Oh no, darling. You're a wonderful lover. This other is part of me too, of who I am, and I want to share it with you."

Her words go a long way toward making me feel better. "So, you trust me."

"Yes. Do *you* trust *me*, Doris Ann?"

The answer comes out automatically. "I trust you, Eleanor."

* * *

So, tonight's the night. I'm on my way to her house to find out about these *activities*. We'd talked it over some the next morning and then she let me stew these past thirty-six hours.

"Eat lightly beforehand and no alcohol," she said. "We can have a glass of wine to relax when you get here, but I don't want you tipsy or numb."

Some relaxing sounds pretty good right now. It's no lie that I trust her, but I'm kind of nervous, just the same. I usually ride my bike, but this evening I walk, wanting a little time to get my head in the right place.

No one can call me a prude or inexperienced, but old-fashioned, Sapphic-style fucking has always been plenty good enough for me. However this is what Ellie wants. I'll do pretty much anything for her.

Everything about the woman is different, a departure from the type I usually date: hard-bodied gym rats. Women like me, in other words. Ellie is curves and dimples and wavy hair. She likes to wear dresses and she's probably the only lesbian in Portland, Oregon without a tattoo. A million freckles, give or take, are enough decoration according to her. I like to play connect the dots with the tip of my tongue, but I keep losing my place and having to start over. Who's in a hurry?

Like anyone who's in love, I could go on about her forever: smart, funny, great cook, lousy athlete—none of which begins to describe her. All these things are glued together with her smile, and how the back of her neck smells, and those honest-to-god come-hither looks she gives me.

The saying goes that opposites attract. Maybe, but I couldn't say what she sees in me. We complement each other; that's the way she puts it. Ellie's good with words. All I know for sure is that colors are brighter and food tastes better since I met her. Whenever I see her, I get a jolt of pride and happiness, not to mention surprise, that this woman picked *me*.

Feeling like it's our first date all over again, I knock at the door.

She looks pretty, and pretty normal, in a silky

camisole and matching loose shorts. A pink scarf tied around her waist pulls the fabric taut. She's not wearing a bra, and I can hardly take my eyes off the heavy sway of her breasts. A tickly warmth kindles between my legs. This is so not what I was expecting—and she knows it.

"Disappointed that it's not black leather?" It's a rhetorical question. Her expression is pleasant, completely ordinary, but her eyes glitter with excitement. It's contagious.

"Let's, uh, skip the wine and just get on with things," I say, and Ellie gestures toward the bedroom. The room looks like it always does, nothing remotely boudoir or dungeon-like.

"Get undressed." Her voice is even and calm, but doesn't invite discussion. I sidle into the corner, toe off my Tevas and start yanking at the pearl snaps of my shirt.

"Slowly."

She's right. Even though I'm impatient to find out what's in store, I don't want to rush through any of it. It isn't just about humoring my girlfriend anymore.

It's hard to remove an exercise bra seductively, but I do my best. The cotton shorts go easier because they roll. Funny how extra naked I feel. She's wearing what amounts to lingerie, but I'm bare, exposed.

The bed—her grandmother's—is an elaborate, wrought iron thing and takes up most of the space in the room. I always figured she kept it out of sentiment, but now I can see the advantages of such a sturdy piece of furniture. It's stripped down to the fitted sheet. At her command, I stretch out. My heart beats faster as she slips fabric loops over my wrists. I suppress a flinch at the rip-tear sound of Velcro fastenings being adjusted near my ear. As she works, Ellie's luscious boobs are practically in my face, under their covering of silk. Mouth watering, I make to nip at them as if this were any regular night.

"Mind." She doesn't raise her voice or frown, still

using that composed tone, but something makes me instantly obey. My ankles are next. I tug at the bonds, testing them. Nope, not going anywhere. She gives a little smirk at my immobility. Getting into the spirit, I pull harder and widen my eyes in play fear. Perhaps that's carrying things a bit far.

"Close your eyes." Of course, that would be part of it.

Fingertips meander a trail up my leg, from the ankle to the back of the knee and the inner thigh, but the touch skirts around my pussy. *Tease.* Now comes a fluttering like butterfly wings over my breasts and up my throat, followed by a silky slither across my face. The scarf, I guess. The fabric covers my eyes and the knot goes at the side where it won't be a lump under my head, a detail that speaks of practice.

You always hear that the loss of one sense heightens the others—my skin sparks with awareness and my ears twitch like a cat's on a stormy night, the sheet smells of sun and wind. This lack of sight gives me permission to unhook the mind and simply feel. I get a mental flash of myself naked, staked out, the patterned band of silk across my face and the dark bush at my crotch. I feel strong and desirable, sexy-brave, for letting my lover have her way with me. A warm hum starts deep in my belly.

There's a shifting of the bed and some soft sounds I can't identify, then the scratch-sputter of a kitchen match with its whiff of sulfur.

A pause…

Fire.

My left nipple is on *fire*.

I hear a thin scream. It's from me. More than the pain, it's the shock that Ellie would really *hurt* me. The thumping of my heart threatens to choke me as my mind scrambles to send the safe word to my mouth, but only a gulping noise comes from my lips—lips that are burning, being touched with something hard, cold, drippy… ice.

"You faker!" I shriek. The response is a wicked chuckle as chill designs, loops and swirls are drawn on my flesh, goose bumps rising in their wake. Ellie is playing a version of the freckle game—she's tracing my tats. Relief sags my body into the pillow top of the mattress.

All the leftover adrenaline has no purpose, and my whole being thrums from the stimulation. I can actually feel each individual pore and follicle. A soft whoosh of breath over the 'burned' breast and the nipple puckers in swift response as teeth worry at the little barbell. My limbs are loose and heavy-light, the internal humming strengthens. I am all skin and eagerness.

Drops of liquid warmth fall on my flesh in a random pattern. Something not-sharp-but-not-dull grazes over me. I follow its path with my mind then the edge is replaced by Ellie's hands. Friction and the heat of her palms melt the soft soy wax as she massages it into my throat, belly, breasts, and arms.

Over the perfume of the candle, I detect the smell of her arousal and I pull again at the restraints, wishing I could do something about it. Normally, I'm the aggressor, proud to take care of my woman, yet it's surprising how much I'm enjoying this, being relieved of the responsibility for my own pleasure. Who knew?

"More, please." Any other time I'd be reluctant to sound so needy, but if Ellie's plan was to make me helpless to desire, she's certainly managed.

"Ah, she wants more, does she?" I don't need to see to tell how much she's enjoying my situation. "Hmmm, where to start?"

Soft and warm, Ellie draws a line with her tongue from the tip of my chin to between my breasts. My belly tightens as she glides down and down to draw open-mouthed, lippy kisses all around my mound. I arch toward her, pussy quivering, so wet I wonder if I'm soaking the sheet. She weaves her fingers through my pubic hair and draws back sharply, a move that bares my clit. Her skillful tongue flicks, teeth nibble, lips suckle until I'm almost sobbing with want. She disengages and moves away.

"Dee?"

I grunt, mute with frustration.

"Do you trust me?"

That question again. A sliver-thin streak of unease stabs the pit of my stomach, but I push it down. I nod.

"Say it."

"Yes, Eleanor, I trust you." My voice is rusty, with an edge.

Movement and fumbling, the sound of a drawer opening and closing, then the scarf is untied. I lie spread-eagled on the bed, my eyes adjusting to the light of the single candle, while my lover kneels between my legs.

She's quite a sight. Naked now, face and throat flushed under the thick scatter of freckles, her hair loosening from its braid. The black harness around her hips is stark against her fair skin. The dildo stands out like a purple flagpole. She holds very still, studying my face, awaiting my reaction. There's a spike of sharp resentment that she's brought me so far only to spring this on me.

Now, it's not as if I don't enjoy penetration, because I do, a lot. We play around with fingers and vibrators and stuff all the time. It's just that when it comes to strapping on, to having, well, intercourse, I'm the dick-*er* rather than the dick-*ee*. I never really thought of doing it any other way.

Ellie waits. She squirts a blob of lube into her palm and strokes the dildo. Her stance is commanding yet relaxed, balanced on her knees, one hand on her hip, but the lusty shine in her eyes begins to cloud as I remain motionless and silent.

"It's up to you, Dee." Her voice is soft, neutral.

Surrender is a word I've always hated, loaded with oppression and exploitation, with weakness. Surrender is so *not butch*—but if I don't give in, then what? By ending this now, what else do I end? Will it be quick, or will our relationship die a slow death? Ellie disappointed, not getting what she wants, me always wondering if I could have satisfied her better, until it finally all dries up and blows away.

"You don't even have to safe-word. Just shake your head no." She's giving me an out, saving my pride if I can't... bring myself to do this thing. I remember being so sure I would do anything for her.

She strokes a finger along my jaw. The essence of tenderness, her gesture says *I will love you anyway.*

This isn't a test. Even if it were, I've already passed. I fill her heart just as she fills mine. The unconditional acceptance melts my resistance as no amount of persuasion ever could. This isn't who's doing what to whom or with what, it's being sexual every way possible with someone I love. Not pushing boundaries, dissolving them.

All this in less time than it takes to blink.

Surrender is easy, the most natural thing in the world.

I *want* my woman to take me however she likes, in any way that pleases her. Emotion clogs my throat. My insides are aching to be filled. Wordless, I nod and raise my hips in invitation.

The leg restraints are loose enough for her to lift my knees a bit and spread my thighs wide, the dildo gently bumping as she gets into position. There's a move of her hand followed by the *burr* of a bullet vibe. I strain my head up to catch a glimpse of Ellie entering me, and my pussy swallowing the purple rod, smooth and broad. She gives an experimental hip movement, then another, before settling into a rhythm.

I am lost in sensations—the sound of her voice and the tug of the fabric cuffs on my wrists, and sharp-sweet pinches on my nipples that send shocks straight to my clit where they blend into the tempo of my lover's borrowed dick. Vibration buzzes out from my core to become part of the cycle. Voice, thrust, tug, buzz.

The momentum builds, like riding an old-timey wooden roller-coaster, with the carriage climbing up and up the big incline, the breath-stopping moment of suspension at the top of the arc, then, inevitably, over. G-force tears a silent scream from me as it lifts me, weightless, and I go flying into space.

I'm on the bed once again with lungs heaving and the sweaty sheet bunched up under my back.

She leans forward, palms on either side of my head. Her breasts are hanging in my face and at last I can feast on her lushness. My pinioned hands flex, wanting to be filled, but I settle for strong, noisy sucking, the way she likes. Her gaze is locked on the working of my mouth and her pelvis starts to writhe, circling the dildo inside me. My walls give a fluttery clench in response and I moan around the mouthful of boob. She jerks away, her nipple leaving my lips with a *pop*.

Ellie rises on her knees, cupping my butt cheeks for leverage. She starts to pound, each thrust surprising an "*Oh!*" of pleasure from me. Her eyes are hazy, but her expression is stern with inner focus as she rides me, jerking my whole body up and down on the mattress, the bonds alternately tightening and loosening. My heart and chest and being open, I want *all* of her inside me, not just the piece of silicone that I attached so much importance to. I buck my hips, silently asking for deeper and harder.

One hand presses on the o-ring of the harness, steadying it and snugging the dildo's flange against her pussy. It's a move I've made so many times to increase the pressure on the mons as I push into her with the rise and fall of the bullet's vibration resonating through the pubic bone. She's feeling what I always feel. The intimacy takes my breath away.

Ellie's flush spreads and deepens, all her rich curves move in time to her thrusts. She arches back as her face contorts in the primal beauty of release with furrowed brows and squinched eyes, her mouth an elongated oval as she cries out.

She crumples forward to rest her forehead against mine, weight on her elbows. Her breath is sweet on my face. She's still panting as she rips the cuffs from my wrists and ankles, pressing a kiss on each in turn as she praises my responsiveness and courage.

Now is the time of whispers and sighs, kisses and half-formed endearments. Drying sweat sticks us together and we giggle whenever we need to move.

"What would your grandmother say about how we're using her bed?"

"You didn't know Gran!"

After a while, Ellie suggests we go again, any way I like. I want to—oh, how I want to—but tonight's revelations and sensations have drained me. I pull her to nestle beside me, almost asleep as I murmur an apology.

"No worries, love. But, um, taking turns is only fair, you know."

"Huh?" Her words penetrate my drowsy state.

"Next time, you get to think up a game for us to play."

My eyes pop open.

Uh-oh.

ABOUT THE EDITOR

CHEYENNE BLUE's erotic fiction has been included in over 90 erotic anthologies since 2000, including *Summer Love: Lesbian Stories of Holiday Romance*, *Best Lesbian Erotica*, *Best Women's Erotica*, *All You Can Eat: a buffet of lesbian romance and erotica*, and *Wild Girls, Wild Nights*. She is the editor of *Forbidden Fruit: stories of unwise lesbian desire* (Ladylit) which is a Lambda Literary Award finalist and a Golden Crown Literary Award finalist. Her collected lesbian short fiction is published by Ladylit as *Blue Woman Stories*—volumes 1 to 3, with more to come. Under her own name she has written travel books and articles, and edited anthologies of local writing in Ireland. She has lived in the U.K., Ireland, the United States, and Switzerland, but now writes, runs, makes bread and cheese, and drinks wine by the beach in Queensland, Australia. Check out her blog at cheyenneblue.com, on Twitter at @IamCheyenneBlue and on Goodreads at goodreads.com/CheyenneBlue.

ABOUT THE AUTHORS

HARPER BLISS (harperbliss.com) is the author of the novels *At the Water's Edge* and *Once in a Lifetime*, the *High Rise* series, the *French Kissing* serial and several other lesbian erotica and romance titles. She is the co-founder of Ladylit, an independent press focusing on lesbian fiction. Harper lives on an outlying island in Hong Kong with her wife and, regrettably, zero pets.

ROSIE BOWER has always been a writer, though she has no fidelity to any particular genre or style. She has come a long way from pre-adolescent fan fiction about beloved cartoon characters, via dramatic teen poetry, and now counts herself as an adult writer, in more ways than one.

JILLIAN BOYD has been blogging about sex, love and relationships (as well as the general weird observations she tends to make) since 2011. She's also the author of a host of erotic short stories, and hopes to be the author of quite a few more. In addition to this, she's edited two erotica anthologies around themes close to her heart—the Roaring Twenties and the thrills of espionage. Curiosity is her greatest driver, along with caffeine and an open mind.

EMILY L. BYRNE lives in lovely Minneapolis with her wife and the two cats that own them. She toils in corporate IT when not writing or reveling in geeky things. Her stories have or will appear in *Bossier, Spy Games, Forbidden Fruit: Stories of Unwise Lesbian Desire, The Princess's Bride,* and *The Mammoth Book of Uniform Erotica.* She blogs at: writeremilylbyrne.blogspot.com and can be found on Twitter at @EmilyLByrne.

VANESSA DE SADE is a forty-something lady who likes to write erotic tales about real women exploring the darker regions of their own sexuality. As well as contributing to anthologies she is the author of the novels *Jane* and *Maid for Milking,* and the solo short story collections *Fur, Black & White Movies, Nude Shots, In the Forests of the Night,* and *Tales from a Tangled Bush.*a

JEREMY EDWARDS (jeremyedwardserotica.com) is the author of some one hundred fifty erotic short stories and two erotocomedic novels, including *The Pleasure Dial: An Erotocomedic Novel of Old-Time Radio.* His work has been published by *Black Heart, Clean Sheets,* Cleis Press, *FeatherLit, Fishnet,* HarperCollins UK, *Meat for Tea,* Penguin, Seal Press, Simon & Schuster, and Vagabondage Press, and in five volumes of *The Mammoth Book of Best New Erotica.* Jeremy has been a featured reader at In the Flesh and Essensuality in New York, the Erotic Literary Salon in Philadelphia, and Arts Night Out Northampton (Massachusetts).

TAMSIN FLOWERS has been writing erotica for three years. She started out with short stories and has featured in more than 20 anthologies to date from Cleis Press, Go Deeper Press, House of Erotica, Xcite Books, and Velvet Books. Her works have featured in collections curated by some of today's most celebrated editors—including Violet Blue (*Best Women's Erotica 2014* and *2015*), Rachel Kramer Bussel (*The Big Book of Submission: 69 Kinky Tales*), Alison Tyler (*Twisted: Bondage with an Edge, Bound for*

Trouble: BDSM for Women) and Kristina Wright (*Best Erotic Romance 2014* and *2015, Passionate Kisses: Erotic Romance Fantasies for Couples*). She has also self-published a sizzling collection of zombie erotica, *Zombie Erotoclypse*, and has had novels and novellas released by Xcite Books (*The Christmas Tattoo, Her Boss and His Client*), Secret Cravings (*The Crimson Bond, The Scarlet Bond*) and Totally Bound *(Doing It for the Coach)*.

SACCHI GREEN (sacchi-green.blogspot.com) is a writer and editor of erotica and other stimulating genres. Her stories have appeared in scores of publications, and she's also edited nine lesbian erotica anthologies, including Lambda Award winners *Lesbian Cowboys* and *Wild Girls, Wild Nights*, both from Cleis Press. A collection of her own work, *A Ride to Remember*, has been published by Lethe Press. Sacchi lives in western Massachusetts, gets away to the mountains of New Hampshire as often as she can, and makes regular forays to NYC for readings and cavorting with her writer friends

ANNABETH LEONG wears high heels and frequents the former haunts of H.P. Lovecraft. One month, she is a baseball fanatic, and the next she's reading about squid. She is frequently confused about her sexuality, but enjoys searching for answers. Her work appears in more than 50 anthologies, including *Best Bondage Erotica* 2013, 2014, and 2015 and *Summer Love: Stories of Lesbian Holiday Romance*. Her latest erotic novel is *Untouched*, from Sweetmeats Press. Find Annabeth online at annabetherotica.com, and on Twitter @AnnabethLeong

ANDI MARQUETTE is an award-winning author of romance, mysteries, and science fiction. Her latest publications include the novel *From the Hat Down* and her co-edited anthology *All You Can Eat: A Buffet of Lesbian*

Romance and Erotica, which is a Lambda finalist. You can find out more about her writing at andimarquette.com.

BRENDA MURPHY writes short stories and novels. She is a member of RWA. Her non-fiction work has been published in edited collections. When she is not writing or cooking, she works as a registered nurse. She lives with an unrepentant parrot and her family in a small town in Ohio. She writes about life, books, and writing on her blog writingwhiledistracted.com. She shares recipes and celebrates food on her blog quinbykitchensideshow.com.

IVY NEWMAN is an Irish student studying English, hoping to help bring queer writing to the foreground. She has a profound weakness for peanut butter and gets all her best ideas in the shower. It makes for very soggy journals.

CELA WINTER took up writing after a career as a restaurant chef. Really. Her erotic fiction has been published in print and on the web. She lives on the fringe of Portland OR, where she is working on a novel—when the Muse isn't distracting her with short story ideas. Find her at celawinter.com.

ALLISON WONDERLAND will be the first to tell you that she loves lesbian literature. She has contributed to over 30 such anthologies, including *Forbidden Fruit, Summer Love, Myth and Magic,* and *First Time for Everything*. Besides being a Sapphic storyteller, Allison is a reader of stories Sapphics tell and enjoys everything from pulp fiction to historical fiction. Find out what else she's into and up to at aisforallison.blogspot.com.

Made in the USA
Charleston, SC
23 October 2015